GW01150008

LITTLE BOOK OF
SECRET AGENTS

Liam McCann

LITTLE BOOK OF
SECRET AGENTS

First published in the UK in 2015

© Demand Media Limited 2015

www.demand-media.co.uk

All rights reserved. No part of this work may be reproduced or utilised in any form or by any means, electronic or mechanical, including photocopying, recording or by any information storage and retrieval system, without prior written permission of the publisher.

Printed and bound in Europe

ISBN 978-1-910540-35-0

The views in this book are those of the author but they are general views only and readers are urged to consult the relevant and qualified specialist for individual advice in particular situations.

Demand Media Limited hereby exclude all liability to the extent permitted by law of any errors or omissions in this book and for any loss, damage or expense (whether direct or indirect) suffered by a third party relying on any information contained in this book.

All our best endeavours have been made to secure copyright clearance for every photograph used but in the event of any copyright owner being overlooked please address correspondence to Demand Media Limited.
Waterside Chambers, Bridge Barn Lane, Woking, Surrey, GU21 6NL.

Contents

04 – 05	Introduction
06 – 08	Aldrich Ames
09 – 13	The Cambridge Five
14 – 16	Eddie Chapman
17 – 27	The CIA
28 – 35	The FBI
36 – 38	Klaus Fuchs
39 – 41	Juan Pujol Garcia
42 – 43	Oleg Gordievsky
44 – 48	Hans Gundelach and Wilhelm Mörz
49 – 51	Robert Hanssen
52 – 58	Soviet Military Intelligence
59 – 60	Doctor Humam Khalil Al-Balawi
61 – 62	Nathan Hale
63 – 64	Virginia Hall
65 – 67	Mata Hari
68 – 71	Alexander Litvinenko
72 – 85	MI5 and MI6
86 – 92	Mossad
93 – 94	Melita Norwood
95 – 98	The NSA
99 – 100	Arthur Owens
101 – 102	Oleg Penkovsky
103 – 104	Dušan Popov
105 – 107	Sidney Reilly
108 – 110	Julius and Ethel Rosenberg
111 – 115	Frederick Rutland and William Forbes-Sempill
116 – 119	The Secret Service
120 – 122	Richard Sorge
123 – 127	James Bond

Chapter 1

Introduction

Many of us have grown up with James Bond, Jason Bourne and Jack Ryan as our heroes, but these spies live and work in a fictional world that bears little resemblance to reality. Secret agents have existed for as long as humans have been in conflict, and this book tells the stories of the people and agencies responsible for some of the most daring and disastrous exploits in the history of intelligence gathering, warfare and espionage.

We'll examine the lives of Nathan Hale, the man executed by the British during the American Revolutionary War; Sidney Reilly, Ace of Spies; and Aldrich Ames,

INTRODUCTION

the man who betrayed countless CIA officers and operations to the Soviet Union. We'll also look at the lesser-known events surrounding the disappearance of Wilhelm Mörz, the only German spy thought to have escaped from Britain during the Second World War, and Mata Hari, the femme fatale who extracted secrets from both sides during World War One.

The agencies behind these men and women will also be examined in detail, and no book on secret agents would be complete without paying tribute to the most famous spy on the silver screen: James Bond.

OPPOSITE LEFT Ian Fleming's original sketch of 007

OPPOSITE RIGHT A statue of Nathan Hale

ABOVE INSET Sidney Reilly

ABOVE Mata Hari in 1906

Chapter 2

Aldrich Ames

Ames was born in Wisconsin in May 1941. His father, Carleton, worked for the CIA's Directorate of Operations at Langley, Virginia, but he was soon posted to Southeast Asia. He was a poor field agent, however, and was recalled to headquarters after three years. Aldrich followed his father into the agency and worked as a low-ranking records analyst.

He rose slowly up the ranks and received good performance reviews so he was eventually accepted to the Career Trainee Program. He married fellow officer Nancy Segebarth and was then posted to Turkey to recruit Soviet intelligence officers as double agents. His reviews were mixed but he eventually returned to New York in 1976 to handle two Soviet assets.

He was a heavy drinker and was responsible for several security breaches, including having affairs while posted in Mexico City. Despite this, he was assigned to Soviet counterintelligence in Washington in 1983, although by then his marriage was over and the divorce settlement was threatening to bankrupt him. This financial uncertainty forced him to consider working for the Russians.

Two years later he passed low-level information to the Soviet Embassy and received $50,000 in return. Having realised he could make a fortune, he began passing more sensitive information to the Russians, particularly the identities of those CIA assets who might discover his espionage activity. When American

RIGHT Aldrich Ames after his arrest

ALDRICH AMES

agents began to disappear, the CIA discounted Ames as the source of the leak and concentrated on Soviet listening devices and potential code breaches.

When the CIA did eventually realise they had a mole, they blamed former agent Ed Howard, but, when another three assets he didn't know were eliminated, suspicion shifted elsewhere. (Howard would eventually defect to the Soviet Union in 1985, partly over his disappointment at the way he'd been treated by his CIA handlers.) Ames enjoyed access to extremely sensitive material on double agents in Rome and in the USA, but it took until 1990 before Paul Redmond's team realised Ames was living well beyond the means of officers on his salary (the Soviets had thus far paid him $4.6 million) and placed him under surveillance.

Ames passed two polygraph tests simply by relaxing but the CIA's surveillance operation was stepped up and he was eventually arrested in 1994. He was sentenced to life in prison after admitting that he had compromised virtually all of the CIA's double agents working within the Soviet Union – at least 10 of whom were executed – and had leaked details of more than 100 intelligence operations.

ALDRICH AMES

WANTED BY THE FBI

ESPIONAGE; INTERSTATE FLIGHT - PROBATION VIOLATION
EDWARD LEE HOWARD

FBI No. 720 744 CA2

Photograph taken 1983

Aliases: Patrick Brian, Patrick M. Brian, Patrick M. Bryan, Edward L. Houston, Roger H. Shannon

DESCRIPTION

Date of Birth:	October 27, 1951	Hair:	brown
Place of Birth:	Alamogordo, New Mexico	Eyes:	brown
Height:	5'11"	Complexion:	medium
Weight:	165 to 180 pounds	Race:	white
Build:	medium	Nationality:	American

Occupations: economic analyst, former U.S. Government employee
Remarks: knowledgeable in the use of firearms
Scars and Marks: 2 inch scar over right eye, scar on upper lip
Social Security Number Used: 457 92 0226
NCIC: D054071919110810 1419
Fingerprint Classification: 4 0 1 R IIO 19
S 17 U IIO

CRIMINAL RECORD

HOWARD HAS BEEN CONVICTED OF ASSAULT WITH A DEADLY WEAPON.

CAUTION

HOWARD SHOULD BE CONSIDERED ARMED AND DANGEROUS AND SHOULD BE APPROACHED WITH CAUTION INASMUCH AS HE HAS BEEN CONVICTED OF ASSAULT WITH A DEADLY WEAPON AND IS PRESENTLY ON SUPERVISED PROBATION.

A Federal warrant was issued on September 23, 1985, at Albuquerque, New Mexico, charging Howard with Espionage (Title 18, U.S. Code, Section 794 (c)). A Federal warrant was also issued on September 27, 1985, at Albuquerque, charging Howard with Unlawful Interstate Flight to Avoid Confinement – Probation Violation (Title 18, U.S. Code, Section 1073).

IF YOU HAVE ANY INFORMATION CONCERNING THIS PERSON, PLEASE CONTACT YOUR LOCAL FBI OFFICE. TELEPHONE NUMBERS AND ADDRESSES OF ALL FBI OFFICES LISTED ON BACK.

William H Webster
DIRECTOR
FEDERAL BUREAU OF INVESTIGATION
UNITED STATES DEPARTMENT OF JUSTICE
WASHINGTON, D. C. 20535
TELEPHONE: 202 324-3000

Entered NCIC
Wanted Flyer 524
October 4, 1985

RIGHT The FBI's Wanted Poster for Ed Howard

Chapter 3

The Cambridge Five

The Cambridge Five were Soviet spies recruited by the KGB's Arnold Deutsch just before the Second World War. Although the identity of the fifth member of the spy ring is still disputed, he was most likely John Cairncross. The others were Guy Burgess, Kim Philby, Donald MacLean and Anthony Blunt. Theodore Maly and Alexander Orlov worked as their case officers.

Having graduated from Cambridge, Philby was recruited by MI6 and assigned to Albania, Istanbul and then Washington as a liaison officer between British and American intelligence. He lived with Burgess in the USA and they along with Blunt began passing sensitive NATO material from the Foreign

Kim Philby

THE CAMBRIDGE FIVE

Office to the Soviet Union. MacLean, meanwhile, served on the Committee for Atomic Development, and he also passed on information about the West's nuclear programme.

In 1949, Philby intercepted a signal from the US's top-secret Venona counterintelligence project and realised that British intelligence had identified MacLean as a double agent. He asked Burgess to return to Britain to warn MacLean, but Burgess panicked and both he and MacLean fled to Moscow. Suspicion now fell on Philby as he was living with Burgess and must have warned him about the intercepted signal. Philby denied the accusations but was discharged from MI6, although he was soon cleared by Foreign Secretary Harold Macmillan and re-employed by the security services. However, the Venona intercepts proved he was the 'third man' in the ring. He was confronted again but fled to the Soviet Union on a freighter before he could be arrested.

An American student at Cambridge called Michael Straight then came forward to say that Anthony Blunt had tried to recruit him. Blunt was brought in for

LEFT Donald MacLean aged 22 in 1935

THE CAMBRIDGE FIVE

THE CAMBRIDGE FIVE

questioning and confessed in return for immunity from prosecution. He named John Cairncross as the fifth member of the ring but there were certainly others, and clouds of suspicion still hang over Sir Roger Hollis (a former Director of MI5), intelligence officer Guy Lidell, Nathaniel Rothschild, Peter Ashby, Leo Long, Lewis Daly and Brian Symon.

The lives of the five proved remarkably unglamorous after their exposure: the KGB refused to employ Philby and he spiralled into a life of drinking and womanising. He ended up having an affair with MacLean's wife and died in 1988. Burgess was a homosexual so his life in the Soviet Union, a country notorious for its persecution of gay people, was extremely miserable. He also drank himself to death at the age of just 52. It took until 1979 before Margaret Thatcher finally released documents on Anthony Blunt. He was shunned by society and died a recluse. MacLean enjoyed life in Moscow and was decorated for his services to the Soviet Union. He died aged 69 in 1983. Cairncross was sacked from the civil service and ended up working for the UN in Rome. He eventually returned to Britain but died in 1995.

The spy ring may have achieved mythical status but recently declassified Soviet documents revealed that their handlers believed them to be unreliable drunks who could barely keep secrets when intoxicated and had almost blown each other's cover on several occasions.

LEFT Anthony Blunt in 1979

BELOW John Cairncross was thought to be the fifth member of the spy ring

Eddie Chapman

Chapman was born in County Durham in 1914. He was a bright child but had little parental guidance and developed a rebellious streak. He joined the Coldstream Guards at the age of 17 but ran away with a girl from Soho. The army eventually tracked him down and sentenced him to three months in a military prison.

On his release, he worked low-paid jobs in London but soon turned to a life of petty crime, safecracking and blackmail to fund a more lavish lifestyle. He was caught committing a burglary on Jersey and was still incarcerated on the island when it was occupied by the Germans during the Second World War. Chapman approached his captors and suggested working for them against the British. He was immediately transferred to Paris and trained in explosives, parachute jumping and espionage by Stephan von Gröning, Head of the Abwehr (German Military Intelligence) in Nantes.

Chapman parachuted into Cambridgeshire in December 1942, his mission being to sabotage Mosquitoes at the De Havilland aircraft factory in Hatfield. As the British had broken the German Enigma Code, they quickly tracked him down and, after interrogation at Latchmere House, Chapman agreed to act as a double agent. He and his handlers added fake damage to the factory, which was then photographed by German reconnaissance aircraft, convincing them that Chapman's mission had been a success.

The Germans asked him to make

RIGHT Chapman's fiancée Dagmar Lahlum worked for the Norwegian Resistance

FAR RIGHT Eddie Chapman was known by the codename Zigzag

EDDIE CHAPMAN

his way to Lisbon for extraction. Once there, he suggested they try to blow up the British ship *City of Lancaster*. The Germans agreed but Chapman simply handed the explosives to the captain so they could be analysed by the British. The crew then staged a mock inspection of the 'damage' to fool the watching Germans.

While teaching German agents spying techniques in Oslo later that year, Chapman was awarded the Iron Cross for the De Havilland and *City of Lan-*

EDDIE CHAPMAN

caster operations, the first such double agent to be recognised since the Franco-Prussian War of 1870. They also gave him 110,000 Reichsmarks and a yacht. In return, he was gathering information on German agents in Norway and sending it back to Britain.

Towards the end of the war, Chapman was sent back to London and tasked with recording where the V-1 bombs were landing. He reported they were striking targets in the city centre when they were actually falling up to 20 miles short. He then inexplicably returned to his criminal past so MI5 were forced to dismiss him.

After the war, he remained friends with von Gröning and he flitted in and out of public life when several books about his exploits were published. Films based on his biography were also released. He died of heart failure in 1997.

BELOW HMS Burwell was a sister ship to the Lancaster

Chapter 5

The CIA

The Central Intelligence Agency is a branch of the US government that collects, processes and analyses foreign intelligence. The intelligence community working for the agency report to the Director of National Intelligence, and it is the only American agency to carry out covert missions.

The attack on Pearl Harbor in December 1941 highlighted the importance of infiltrating enemy intelligence networks to gather information about their objectives. In the immediate aftermath of the Second World War, agencies such as the FBI, State Department and War Department all wanted extra powers, but the head of the Office of Strategic Services, General William Donovan, wrote to President Roosevelt in 1944 and proposed forming a Central Intelligence Service that would recruit personnel from all the other agencies, including his own. The OSS had been modelled on the British Secret Intelligence Service (MI6) and the Special Operations Executive so it was a formidable organisation by the end of the war.

Donovan wanted his operatives to be able to gather intelligence overtly and covertly to determine national intelligence objectives, correlate material collected, and carry out subversive missions at home and abroad. The FBI then conducted a study into the OSS but, as the new CIS would be a rival for its power and budget, the report only praised a few minor operations – like rescuing downed pilots from behind enemy lines – and otherwise condemned its influ-

THE CIA

ABOVE The headquarters of the Central Intelligence Agency in Langley, Virginia

ence and capability as an intelligence-gathering entity.

President Truman was doubtless swayed by the FBI's report as the OSS saw its numbers cut by 85% – down to just 2,000 personnel – in the first two weeks after Japan's surrender. By October 1945, the OSS had been split into three departments, but this restructuring only lasted until the end of the year. In January 1946, Truman renamed the organisation the National Intelligence Authority, but this lasted less than two years.

The Central Intelligence Agency only came into being in July 1947 when President Truman signed the National Security Act. As there was no congressional mandate, however, Lawrence Houston helped amend the act, and the National Security Council and CIA were formally established on September 18. It would

THE CIA

take another two years before the Central Intelligence Agency Act exempted it from the limitations of federal funding and authorised its officers to use confidential intelligence-gathering techniques.

At first, the reports that came in were confusing and the agency took its time establishing protocols that aided organisation and efficiency. In fact the CIA initially found itself producing little intelligence of value and it was all but powerless during North Korea's invasion of their southern neighbours in 1950. Truman acted quickly, however, and he appointed Walter Bedell Smith as Director of the CIA to address these shortcomings.

As the CIA still answered to Truman, the Secretary of Defense and the State Department, Smith found himself being tossed around between the White House, a lukewarm FBI and the Pentagon. He turned to Sidney Souers and General Hoyt Vandenburg for help and they suggested concentrating on gathering as much information about the USSR as possible. More than 200 field agents in Germany, Austria, Switzerland and Eastern Europe were then assigned to the task, although they soon stumbled across the biggest hurdle they and every other clandestine agency faced: separating truth from fiction.

As if this didn't present the fledgling agency with enough problems, the CIA was then authorised to carry out covert operations against enemy states or groups so long as responsibility for such action could not be attributed to the United States. To legislate for this, an Office of Policy Coordination was created, although this further confused matters when the head of the OPC re-

BELOW Each star on the memorial wall represents a fallen CIA officer

THE CIA

BELOW The CIA covered up the loss of Gary Powers' U-2 spyplane in 1960

fused to report to the CIA, and stations abroad were often manned by personnel from both – competing – groups.

In an era when international relations between the East and West were cooling rapidly, several countries were developing the bomb, and war was raging in the Far East, the CIA was thrown in at the deep end. Things were made worse when Kim Philby, a British liaison officer with the CIA, leaked details of countless British and American operations to the Russians. When Bill Weisband was also found to be passing decrypted codes to the Soviets, it seemed as if the CIA's shelf-life was about to expire.

However, developments in cryptanalysis and a newfound ability to rig foreign

THE CIA

elections (notably in Italy when American funds bought the Christian Democrats victory and prevented the leftist coalition gaining power and possibly allying with the Soviet Union) proved the CIA could influence world events. More failures in Korea and China were followed by a smooth, if rather complicated, transfer of power in Iran after the assassination of Prime Minister Haj Ali Razmara. This led to the Anglo-Iranian Oil Company being nationalised, removing British influence in the area – as well as a huge source of income for the West – so the CIA and the British Secret Intelligence Service launched Operation Ajax to overthrow new Prime Minister Mohammed Mosaddegh.

Secretary of State John Dulles and his brother Allen, then head of the CIA, drafted a plan to remove Mosaddegh. The Shah of Iran initially refused to sanction the plan but he was bribed into dismissing Modaddegh in favour of General Fazlollah Zahedi in August 1953. The Shah then fled to Rome to avoid the bloodshed but Zahedi was eventually installed as the new Prime Minister. He immediately agreed to re-supply the world – particularly the US and UK – with Iranian oil. More than 300 people were killed during the transition and many more of Mosaddegh's supporters were convicted and executed in the aftermath of the coup.

The CIA also ran operations in Guatemala to install the sympathetic Carlos Castillo Armas as president, then helped overthrow Soviet puppet Patrice Lumumba in Congo, and also covered up the shooting down of Gary Powers's

BELOW Oliver North prepares to give evidence regarding the sale of arms in the Middle East

THE CIA

ABOVE The damage to the USS Cole from the suicide attack in 2000 is clearly visible

U-2 spyplane over Russia in 1960. The following year, the CIA turned its attention to the overthrow of Fidel Castro in Cuba but the invasion at the Bay of Pigs was a tactical and operational disaster for President Kennedy as the dissident Cubans working with the CIA eventually backed out of the deal and were defeated by forces loyal to Castro.

In October 1962, the island once again became the centre of attention as U-2 images showed Russian ballistic missiles being deployed 90 miles from the US coast. Kennedy acted on the CIA's intelligence and eventually forced Nikita Krushchev to withdraw Soviet weapons from Cuba.

The CIA ran countless operations during the Vietnam War but their agents in North Vietnam were largely ineffective. JFK demanded results but, after his assassination in November 1963, President Lyndon Johnson backed intelligence gathering over covert action and the agency's influence in the area declined. Their assessment that 500,000 troops were still available to the north contradicted the army's estimate of

THE CIA

fewer than 300,000 so the war dragged on as the US pushed for victory. It was an ill-advised failure.

When Nixon's men – all former CIA officers – broke into the Watergate building to steal information about his political rivals, the president tried to blame the CIA, stating that if Director Richard Helms took the fall, every tree in the forest would follow. He also tried to use the CIA to disrupt the FBI investigation. After his re-election, he again stated his desire to ruin the CIA and install James Schlesinger as director of a new Foreign Service, which would be monitored by Henry Kissinger.

Schlesinger grew suspicious of Nixon, however, so he asked every domestic CIA employee to provide him with details about intelligence that had been gathered using techniques that weren't permitted by the agency's charter. The resulting 693-page report was passed from Schlesinger to new director William Colby. It listed everything that had been ascertained illegally and became known as the Family Jewels: imprisonment of KGB defectors, wiretapping members of the anti-war movement, surveillance of American journalists, illegal break-ins, opening celebrity mail, conducting non-consensual human experiments, and aiding political assassinations, amongst others.

It emerged that the CIA had also withheld Watergate documents, infiltrated several of the US government's agencies to gather intelligence on corruption and homeland security, and

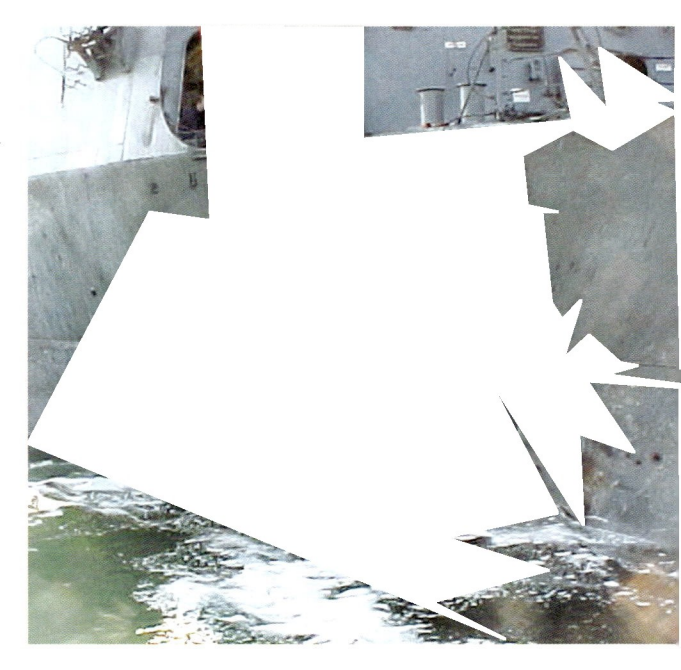

BELOW Seventeen US servicemen were killed in the attack

THE CIA

used the American mafia to try to assassinate Fidel Castro on several occasions. When this information was released in 2007, Attorney General Laurence Silberman demanded an investigation into the CIA's activity at home and abroad. After eight such investigations were carried out, a Select Intelligence Committee evolved to supervise covert presidential operations.

Despite their dubious methods of gathering intelligence over the last 40 years, some notable successes have been achieved: Vladimir Vetrov began releasing information to NATO about the Soviet Union's intelligence programmes, so the CIA used him to provide the Russians with disinformation about US shuttle missions, computer software and technological advances. Vetrov's work contributed to several high-profile Soviet failures, from their space programme to the manufacture of their oil pipelines.

The CIA also funded opposition groups in Afghanistan, Iran, Nicaragua and Lebanon, but their position was often compromised and 63 people – including seven CIA officers – were killed when a massive car bomb exploded outside the US Embassy in Beirut in 1983. Another bomb at a nearby American military base killed 242 personnel. At the time, Oliver North was selling weapons to Iran to buy the release of American hostages, but this covert operation exploded spectacularly when the bombs used in both attacks were linked to the Iranians.

The CIA also supplied arms to both sides in the Iran-Iraq War, and its officers then mistakenly reported that the Shiites and Kurds would rise up to overthrow Saddam Hussein if encouraged by

BELOW The aftermath of the 1993 World Trade Centre bombing

the US-led coalition. Saddam brutally crushed the uprisings and remained in power for another decade, after which his nuclear programme was discovered. The CIA had no previous knowledge of this capability despite maintaining a covert presence in Iraq for the duration of Saddam's tenure.

The CIA was also caught short as the Soviet Union began to break up. Most of their officers didn't speak Russian and several had never been to Moscow. Their intelligence was predictably poor as a result. Indeed the three Soviet spies who worked for the CIA in Russia for the duration of the Cold War were all captured and executed. The agency was also unprepared for the bombing of the World Trade Centre in 1993, the American Embassy bombings in Dar es Salaam and Nairobi by Al Qaeda in 1998, and the attack on the USS *Cole* in 2000.

In the immediate aftermath of these failings, the CIA delivered dire warnings to President George W Bush about further Al Qaeda attacks. President Clinton hadn't given the agency much support and had refused to sanction the assassination of Osama Bin Laden. Bush was also against taking him out and believed this to be a case of the boy crying wolf, so the CIA warnings weren't afforded much credibility. Bush still instructed the CIA to apprehend known Al Qaeda sympathisers but they provided little information.

When National Security Coordinator Richard Clarke warned against inaction and issued a risk assessment to Condoleezza Rice, he was also ignored. Within a month, Bin Laden would carry out the worst terrorist attack in history when three hijacked aircraft were crashed into the World Trade Centres in New York and the Pentagon in Washington. A fourth aircraft was prevented from reaching its target by the passengers but it also crashed with the loss of everyone onboard.

All of America's security services were criticised after the attacks that left 2,996 people dead. The CIA had set up a Strategic Assessments Branch in 2001 but it had difficulty recruiting personnel and only appointed a head on September 10. The CIA was running a station at World Trade Centre 7, which was also destroyed in the attacks, and this was also the headquarters of their investigation into criminal terrorism. This is one of the reasons why so many conspiracy theories have sprung up in the years since.

President Bush immediately approved the decision to send CIA para-

THE CIA

military officers into Afghanistan to capture and interrogate Taliban leaders. Prisoners at Qala Jangi Prison overpowered their captors, however, and CIA officer John Spann was beaten to death. As the agency had also sent 12 officers into Iraq, there were fears that their cover would be blown if more agents in Afghanistan were captured alive.

President Bush knew he had to act fast so he decided to 'believe' the weak case for Iraq's weapons of mass destruction and ordered the invasion of Iraq in 2003. Despite the speed of the attack, several officers were exposed, although the remainder were integral to the missions of the 10th Special Forces.

The US-led occupation of Iraq was probably a low point in the history of the organisation but CIA operatives finally captured Khalid Sheik Mohammad and he helped identify one of Bin Laden's couriers. The CIA eventually tracked Bin Laden to a compound in Abbottabad, Pakistan, and they and the Special Forces finally got their man in May 2011. The operation also liberated extensive intelligence about Al Qaeda's plans for the future.

In March 2015, documents were released stating that the CIA would be extensively reformed to bring it into line with more modern intelligence-gathering entities. This involved establishing a digi-

THE CIA

tal directorate to train officers to use the latest technology to counter cyber threats; forming a centre of excellence to develop talent; increasing the size and capability of the CIA University; and restructuring the agency's hierarchy of power.

BELOW The CIA was heavily criticised for not anticipating the attacks on 9/11

Chapter 6

The FBI

The predecessor to the FBI was the National Bureau of Criminal Identification, which was formed in the USA in 1896. This gave domestic intelligence agencies access to known criminals and created an autonomous investigative agency that reported to Attorney General Charles Bonaparte. Personnel were recruited from other agencies, the military and the police, and they collectively became known as special agents.

A Bureau of Investigation followed in July 1908 when Bonaparte selected some of these people to work for the new agency. They initially investigated domestic crime such as prostitution, tax evasion, kidnapping, murder, robbery and organised crime. The first champion of the cause was John Edgar Hoover, who would remain at the helm from 1924 until 1972. He is credited with turning the fledgling organisation into a professional scientific investigative agency, gathering evidence with bugging and wiretapping to convict career criminals.

In the build-up to the Second World War – and in the subsequent Cold War – the FBI proved to be an invaluable asset when investigating domestic terrorism, spying and cryptography. When evidence surfaced that there were several Soviet intelligence officers working within American agencies, particularly the CIA, Hoover became obsessed with eliminating the communist threat.

After Pearl Harbor, thousands of Japanese Americans were rounded up and

THE FBI

LEFT J Edgar Hoover was Director of the FBI for 48 years

THE FBI

RIGHT Martin Luther King makes his 'I have a dream' speech in 1963

OPPOSITE Crime boss Sam Giancana

THE FBI

sent to internment camps. The FBI handled their relocation and placed many under surveillance for the remainder of the war. The bureau was also responsible for investigating civil rights leaders whom Hoover believed to have communist sympathies. He and Martin Luther King Junior ended up in a war of words when King suggested white supremacists were nothing more than terrorists so Hoover branded him the country's most notorious liar. The FBI even sent King a letter encouraging him to commit suicide. In 1971 things got even worse for the bureau when secret documents were stolen indicating that they knew much more about the assassinations of political activists than had been previously thought, and that they had bugged the phones of prominent politicians.

Throughout the 1950s and '60s, the bureau cracked

THE FBI

ABOVE The aftermath of the Waco siege, an event that is said to have influenced Timothy McVeigh to bomb the Alfred Murrah Federal Building in Oklahoma in 1995

down on organised crime, and there were notable successes against crime syndicates run by Sam Giancana, but the FBI made a serious blunder when they allowed four men to be wrongly convicted of murder just to protect a source. The men were eventually awarded $100 million in damages, but by then they'd spent decades in prison.

The 1984 Los Angeles Olympics posed many security questions so, in the post-Hoover era, special weapons

THE FBI

and tactics (SWAT) and hostage rescue teams (HRT) were established. Agents who had been on duty assessing foreign threats were also redeployed to domestic intelligence at the end of the Cold War. This was brought home with the 1993 World Trade Centre bombing and the attack in Oklahoma two years later. The FBI was also fighting on the front line in the Waco siege, after which electronic surveillance was increased.

After the September 11 attacks, the

ABOVE The remains of the federal building where 168 people lost their lives

THE FBI

RIGHT The headquarters of the FBI

FBI's priorities shifted to preventing terrorism, gathering foreign intelligence, cyber security, high-tech crime, corruption, and violent and organised crime. Both the FBI and CIA were criticised for not acting on intelligence before the attacks, and security breaches – such as the Robert Hanssen case – further highlighted the agency's inadequacies.

The FBI is now housed in the J Edgar Hoover Building in Washington, DC, although there are 56 field offices that report to headquarters. The agency recently abandoned a $300-million upgrade to its IT structure, but it does still monitor email and telecommunications across the world. The FBI employs more than 33,000 people today – 13,000 special agents and 20,000 support professionals – all of whom had to pass the bureau's strict mental and physical assessment.

LITTLE BOOK OF **SECRET AGENTS**

Chapter 7

Klaus Fuchs

Emil Julius Klaus Fuchs was born in Rüsselsheim in Germany in 1911. He went to the University of Leipzig in 1930 and studied politics but he then switched to Kiel and devoted his energy to maths and physics. He aligned himself initially with the Social Democratic Party but soon joined the Communist Party of Germany. He fled the city after being attacked by Nazis, but he was also forced to leave the Kaiser Wilhelm Institute for Physics in Berlin when his allegiance became known.

In 1933 he met English couple Ronald and Jessie Gunn at an anti-fascist rally in Paris. They invited him to England and, as they moved in high social circles, arranged for Fuchs to study physics under Nevill Mott at Bristol University. Fuchs was awaiting the result of an application for British citizenship when the Second World War broke out so he was transferred first to the Isle of Man and then to a camp in Sherbrooke in Canada.

A year later he returned to Britain to work with Max Born at Edinburgh University. He published a number of influential papers on theoretical physics and was asked by Rudolf Peierls to join Britain's atomic bomb project, codenamed Tube Alloys. He was promptly granted citizenship and signed the Official Secrets Act declaration.

In 1942, Fuchs contacted Simon Davidovitch Kremer, a Soviet GRU intelligence officer, requesting permission to deliver information via courier to Soviet military intelligence. When Fuchs was sent to New York to work on the Man-

RIGHT Klaus Fuchs in around 1940

KLAUS FUCHS

hattan Project (America's atom bomb), his control passed to the NKGB, the Soviet Union's civilian intelligence agency. He continued to pass secrets to the Russians while working at Los Alamos, and he was one of the 425 people present at the first nuclear 'Trinity' test in New Mexico.

Fuchs remained with the laboratory after the war and continued work on the latest nuclear weapons. Transferring material related to his work out of the country was strictly prohibited but Fuchs kept the British and the Russians up to date on the latest developments as well as the obstacles faced by the Americans. He returned to Britain in 1946 but continued to pass on information regarding the latest hydrogen bombs and producing uranium-235.

Messages decrypted by the Venona Project's counterintelligence officers in 1949 suggested that Fuchs was spying for the Russians, but he didn't admit to providing the Soviets with any sensitive information until a second interview in 1950. He then opened up about his handlers and the courier, although he failed to implicate the Cambridge spy ring of Philby, Burgess, Hunt and MacLean despite the fact that he certainly

KLAUS FUCHS

BELOW In the first moments of the Trinity atom bomb test, the fireball reaches metres 200 metres high

knew Philby and MacLean.

As most of the documents relating to Fuchs's betrayal are still classified, it's difficult to assess the damage he did to the West's nuclear programme. The common consensus is that he made little difference as Soviet research was initially limited by how much uranium they could procure and, by the time he'd left the Americans in 1946, the hydrogen delivery system was still in its infancy.

He was sentenced to 14 years in prison but only served nine. He returned to East Germany in 1959 and published many more notable papers on theoretical physics. He died in Berlin in 1988.

Chapter 8

Juan Pujol Garcia

Juan Pujol was born in Barcelona in 1912. He rebelled at school and eventually took up a post as an apprentice in a hardware shop. He served with the light artillery during his military service but wasn't cut out to be a soldier and refused to fight for the republican government during the Spanish Civil War because of the way they'd treated his family. He deserted to the nationalists but they were equally intolerable and Pujol was left with a vehement distrust of fascism and communism.

At the outbreak of the Second World War, Pujol felt a moral obligation to help the British fight the Nazis. They rejected his approach so he decided to begin espionage work for the Germans

LEFT Juan Pujol in the 7th Light Infantry

ABOVE One of the many inflatable Sherman Tanks that convinced German analysts that the D-Day attack would occur in the Pas de Calais instead of Normandy

before trying to convince the British he would work for them as a double agent. He took a false pro-Nazi Spanish government official's identity and convinced German intelligence officer Friedrich Knappe-Ratey to let him travel to Britain to try to recruit a network of agents.

He instead moved to Lisbon and used a tourist's guide, reference books and news footage to provide his German handlers with detailed information about his time in Britain. His reports back to Knappe-Ratey were intercepted by British code-breakers at Bletchley Park and were so convincing that the British launched an investigation.

When the United States entered the war, Pujol contacted Lieutenant Patrick Demorest in Lisbon and insisted the American navy let the British know what he'd been up to. They finally realised that Pujol had been feeding the Germans disinformation when he sent the Kriegsmarine on a wild-goose chase for a non-existent convoy.

The British brought Pujol and his family to England and they continued to deliver reports – some accurate but of

JUAN PUJOL GARCIA

little value, some valuable but timed to arrive too late to be useful, and some inaccurate – to his handler in Lisbon. The Germans were so impressed with his fictional network of spies that they stopped recruiting agents in Britain.

Pujol and the British made occasional mistakes, such as when one of their 'agents' failed to report ship movements off Liverpool, but Pujol explained the oversight by saying the officer had been compromised and had committed suicide rather than be interrogated. The Germans were even more impressed with the agent's loyalty and started paying his fictional widow a war pension.

As they were supplying the Germans with original coded messages, they were intercepted as a matter of priority when Knappe-Ratey sent them on from Lisbon to Berlin. This allowed the teams at Bletchley Park the perfect opportunity to calibrate their code-breaking equipment as they knew the content of the original message.

Pujol's fictional team proved equally valuable in the build-up to D-Day. He helped convince the Germans that the main attack would take place in the Pas de Calais. Then, when Operation Overlord was launched on June 6, 1944, Pujol sent more messages claiming this was merely a diversion as most of the Allied forces were still massing in Southeast England. The deception was complete when thousands of inflatable tanks, aircraft and military vehicles were photographed by the Germans along the south coast. More than 60 of his reports reached Hitler himself, and the Führer maintained an enormous military presence in the Pas de Calais waiting for an attack that never came. There can be little doubt that Pujol contributed to the overall success of the Normandy Landings and Victory in Europe.

The Germans hailed him a war hero and awarded him the Iron Cross, while the British gave him an MBE. MI5 helped him fake his own death in 1949 in case he was hunted down by surviving Nazis. He lived an unremarkable life thereafter and his exploits were only discovered by British politician Rupert Allason 25 years later. Allason tracked Pujol down to New Orleans in 1984 and convinced him to return to England. He was received by the Duke of Edinburgh at Buckingham Palace and toured the Normandy beaches as part of the 40th anniversary of D-Day shortly afterwards. He died in Caracas in 1988.

Chapter 9

Oleg Gordievsky

Oleg Gordievsky was born in Moscow in 1938 and, having left the state institute, he joined the Foreign Service in East Berlin. Two years later, he was recruited by the KGB and posted to Copenhagen. When the Soviet Union invaded Czechoslovakia in 1968, Gordievsky decided to contact MI6. When the Russians then posted him to London, he had the perfect opportunity to work for the British.

He immediately proved his value by helping to avert nuclear catastrophe in 1983 when the Russians misinterpreted a NATO exercise as a first strike on the Soviet Union. He also notified the British that the more amenable Mikhail Gorbachev would assume office and that peace talks should soon follow.

The Russians eventually realised that Gordievsky was passing information to the British – it's possible that Aldrich Ames was their source – so they recalled him to Moscow and interrogated him for five hours. As he was facing a potential death sentence, the British initiated a daring plan to help him escape. Gordievsky evaded his KGB surveillance officers and fled by train and official British Embassy car to Finland. His wife and children weren't able to join him in England for six years.

In 1995 he claimed in a book that Michael Foot was working for the KGB, for which the former labour leader received a substantial out-of-court settlement. The story refused to die, however, as Gordievsky's information had always been reliable. In 2008 he spent several days in hospital after apparently being poisoned.

LEFT Ronald Reagan thanks Gordievsky for helping to avert nuclear catastrophe during the Operation Able Archer confusion in 1983

ABOVE Oleg Gordievsky is congratulated by Baroness Thatcher in 2007

Chapter 10
Hans Gundelach and Wilhelm Mörz

Hans Gundelach was a Danish engineer and pilot whose exploits read like a boy's own story, but his contribution to the war effort probably wouldn't be known if he hadn't left his diaries to the author's neighbour in 1999.

In April 1940, Gundelach was told by his mother that several Jews were working on a new gun-sight for the U-boats at his family's armament factory in Aachen, Germany. She asked Gundelach to cross the border and try to help the Jews escape, but, as soon as he reached the factory, news filtered through that Germany had invaded Denmark. Gundelach was stranded in Aachen with no hope of making it home.

He was a courageous and resourceful man, so he decided to steal the technical drawings of the gun-sight and try to make it to England. The U-boats were already sinking hundreds of ships in the Atlantic convoys and Britain was running out of food. The new gun-sight would allow the submarines to sink more ships and the war in the West might be lost.

Gundelach made it across the border into occupied France and stumbled across a disused British airfield. All the aircraft had been destroyed on the ground but one Hurricane was just about serviceable. Gundelach repaired the aircraft under the noses of the German patrols and flew across the Channel to England. Having crash-landed at Bodiam Castle, he caught a train to London but, although his English was

RIGHT Colonel Robin Stephens oversaw Gundelach's incarceration at Camp 020

HANS GUNDELACH AND WILHELM MÖRZ

good, he spoke with a slight accent and was unfamiliar with the local customs so he was immediately arrested as a spy.

It was during his first interrogation at Farm Hall in Godmanchester, Cambridgeshire, that he learned about Wilhelm Mörz. Mörz was originally a Hamburg police detective who had joined the Nazi party in January 1933. He soon earned a reputation for double-crossing informants and penetrated anti-Nazi groups of German émigrés in Czechoslovakia. He eventually betrayed them and hundreds were executed. He was also active in Holland, where he betrayed a number of Dutch anti-Nazis. He was even suspected of being the German agent responsible for the infamous Venlo Incident, in which two British intelligence officers were snatched from inside Dutch territory when Abwehr operatives convinced the pair they were anti-Nazis plotting to assassinate Hitler. Mörz was then apparently smuggled into Britain as part of Operation Lena in June 1940.

The spies were told to infiltrate society to make it easier for German forces to invade during Operation Sealion. However, they were poorly trained in the language and customs and all but

HANS GUNDELACH AND WILHELM MÖRZ

BELOW Ned Potter's family were smuggled out of Denmark on the Queen Maud. The ship was later sunk by the U-38 off North Africa

Mörz were captured. A nationwide manhunt was launched to find him and he was spotted in Regent Street in late June, but that was the last confirmed sighting. British records declassified in 2006 claim that Mörz was the only spy to escape capture during the war, but Gundelach's personal account disputes this and sheds new light on Mörz's fate.

Gundelach found it impossible to convince his captors of his story because his spoken German was so good and they believed he was one of the spies sent to England during Operation Lena.

HANS GUNDELACH AND WILHELM MÖRZ

However, Gundelach knew there was someone in the UK who could vouch for his identity. The Gundelachs owned a holiday cottage in Holstebro, Denmark, and their neighbours were half English. Although Gundelach knew the neighbours had been stranded in Denmark after the German invasion, he often played in the street with the family's seven-year-old son, Ned Potter. If the Potters had managed to return to England, little Ned would be able to identify him.

The British looked into his story and discovered that the Potters had been smuggled out of Denmark on the ship *Queen Maud*. They took Gundelach to Latchmere House where he was further interrogated by Lieutenant-Colonel Robin 'Tin-Eye' Stephens before Aase Potter and her son Ned arrived and identified Gundelach as their neighbour in Denmark.

The British immediately realised that Gundelach could be a godsend as all the Germans incarcerated at Latchmere House also believed he was one of the Lena spies. Gundelach agreed to work for the Secret Intelligence Service and he and his handler, 'Stanley', soon had names and addresses of the spies' contacts in the south of England. They believed they'd traced Mörz to a safehouse just north of Brighton but they only captured his contacts and an Enigma machine. However, they also discovered a passport used by Mörz and a lead to the Ship Hotel in Brighton.

Gundelach arranged a meeting and overpowered the German spy before dumping his unconscious body down the hotel's laundry chute to where Stanley was waiting. The pair then drove to a pig farm in Horsham and fed Mörz to the animals.

Gundelach remained in Britain for the rest of the war. He joined the Polish 303 Squadron and then 501 Squadron and flew Hurricanes at the end of the Battle of Britain. He trained pilots until 1944 when MI5 decided the risk of him falling into German hands after the Allied invasion of France was acceptable. His knowledge of the Mörz affair was by then irrelevant. He was posted to an operational squadron flying Hurricanes in a support role over mainland Europe as at this stage of the war the Luftwaffe was just about grounded by a lack of fuel.

Gundelach was killed by a lightning strike on the water off Rügen Island in the Baltic Sea during the summer of

HANS GUNDELACH AND WILHELM MÖRZ

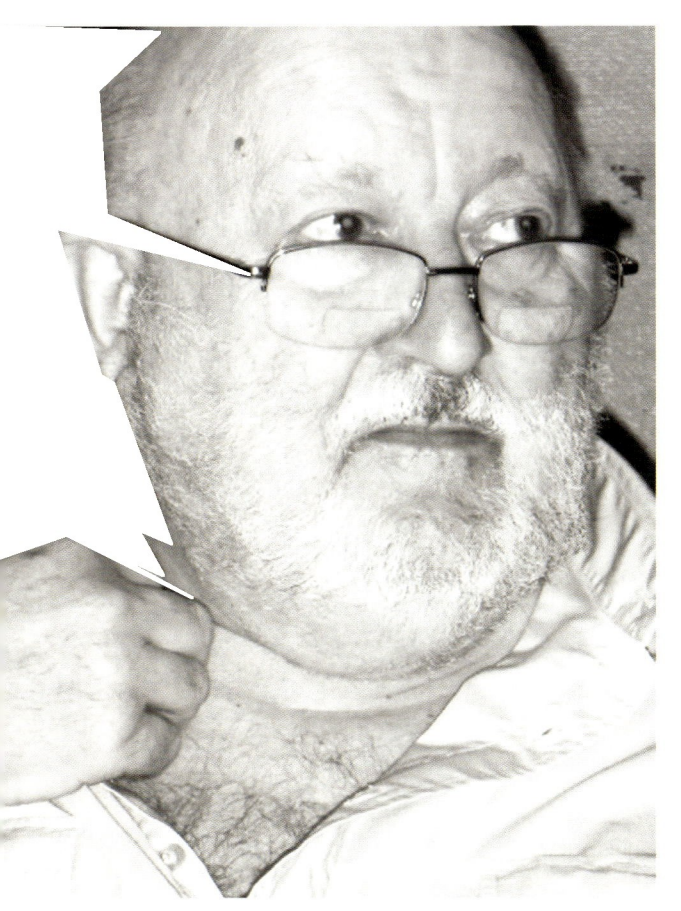

1999. He died doing what he loved more than anything else since he'd retired: teaching young people how to sail.

His story would perhaps not have been written, and would have remained unknown outside his close family, were it not for him leaving his papers, flight logs and a collection of audiotapes to the young man who had identified him at Latchmere House: Ned Potter. Details of his incarceration only came to light with the release of files recently declassified by the British government, and Gundelach's personal papers only give credence to the events described.

His family said he never spoke of his wartime exploits and he confided only in his wife, Louise. He even kept his involvement in the Wilhelm Mörz affair secret to the end. It was, after all, a private crusade to establish his loyalty to the Secret Intelligence Service operatives who had doubted him for so long, and which, in the end, remained unknown except to a tiny group of people. Gundelach's incredible story has recently been dramatised in the novel *The Little English Boy*.

LEFT Ned Potter in 2009

Chapter 11

Robert Hanssen

Robert Hanssen was born in Chicago to a family of Eastern European descent, but he had a poor relationship with his domineering father. He earned a chemistry degree and became interested in Russian but he was overlooked as a cryptographer with the NSA due to budget cuts. He eventually joined the Chicago police as a financial forensic investigator but was asked to join the FBI in 1976.

He soon transferred to Soviet counterintelligence but almost immediately began working for Russian military intelligence, the GRU, with his only apparent motive being money. He gave the Soviets detailed information on the FBI's wiretapping and electronic surveillance and also passed on lists of suspected double agents. He then betrayed CIA informant Dmitri Polyakov who had spent 20 years passing information to the Americans while working as a general in the Soviet military. The Soviets inexplicably didn't arrest Polyakov until he was betrayed a second time by Aldrich Ames. They executed him three years later.

Hanssen's wife, Bonnie, discovered him writing to his handlers in 1981 but he claimed he was only passing on false information. He spent the next four years identifying and capturing Soviet spies in the US, and then evaluating whether they could be turned, and it wasn't until 1985 that he resumed working for the KGB. He gave them the names of another three double agents, but Ames had already betrayed the men so US intelligence

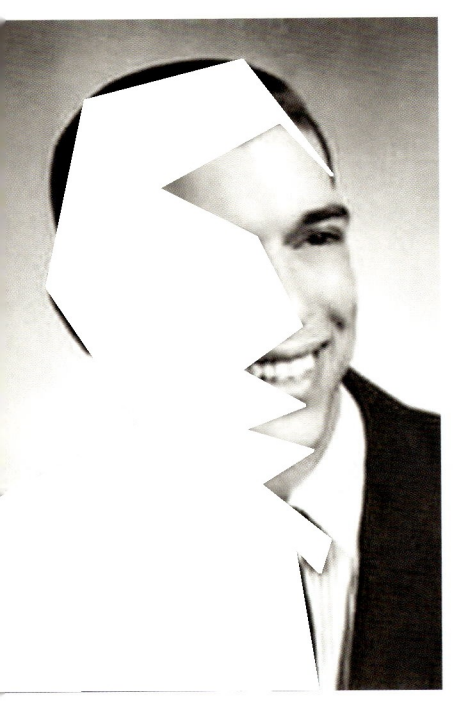

ROBERT HANSSEN

ABOVE Robert Hanssen as a young man

didn't investigate Hanssen.

He continued passing on sensitive information for cash until 1989. He then warned the Russians that the FBI was investigating Felix Bloch, a member of the State Department who had been seen meeting with a known KGB officer. Bloch was never formally charged with spying but the FBI knew they had a mole passing on information to the KGB so they began looking for the traitor. Somewhat coincidentally, they had already asked Hanssen to initiate the probe, but, as he was the man he was supposed to find, it came as no surprise when he came up empty handed. Hanssen's brother-in-law, Mark Wauck also worked for the FBI and he suggested his superiors look into Hanssen but his request was denied.

After the collapse of the Soviet Union, Hanssen took even more risks and once approached a GRU officer in the car park of the Russian Embassy. He then hacked into a colleague's computer, which was traced, but still no action was taken. In 1997, he again hacked into the FBI's high-security network to try to find out if he was under investigation. His probes left footprints in the system but still nothing was done. Having not contacted the Russians for several years, and believing he was still in the clear, Hanssen renewed his relationship with the Russian Foreign Intelligence Service.

The Americans now had Ames in custody but several security breaches couldn't be traced back to the CIA officer so the agency and the FBI teamed up to root out the second mole. They mistakenly arrested Brian Kelley in 1998 and all but ruined his reputation over the next two years.

With the investigation going nowhere, the FBI approached former KGB agents and offered to buy the Russian files relating to the mole. A businessman who still hasn't been named stole the mole's file from KGB headquarters and sold it to the

ROBERT HANSSEN

FBI for $7 million and a new life for his family in the US. The file contained papers and a single audiotape, which finally gave the FBI a name: Robert Hanssen.

The FBI placed him under surveillance and caught him in the act of making another dead drop, although they didn't manage to apprehend his handler, Viktor Cherkashin (who was also Aldrich Ames's case officer). Hanssen was convicted and given 15 consecutive life sentences. He spends 23 hours a day in solitary confinement at a maximum-security penitentiary in Colorado.

BELOW The high-security prison where Hanssen will spend the rest of his life

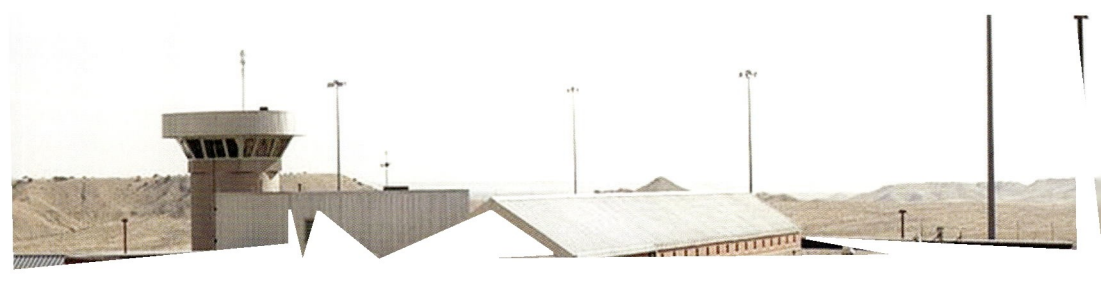

Chapter 12

Soviet Military Intelligence

The Komitet Gosudarstvennoy Bezopasnosti (KGB) was the Soviet Committee for State Security between 1954 and the break up of the union in 1991. The country had a long line of secret police organisations that began with the Cheka, an agency founded in 1917 by Lenin in the aftermath of the Russian Revolution. Its aim was to combat revolution, sabotage, profiteering and corruption.

The Cheka was a brutal organisation that targeted any servicemen suspected of working for Imperial Russia, families of office volunteers, clergymen, anyone who didn't support the Soviet government, and anyone with a net worth of more than 10,000 roubles. It wasn't bound by law and had unlimited powers, so its agents were responsible for thousands of arrests and executions, mostly of deserters from the army during what became known as the Red Terror.

In 1922 the Cheka became the NKVD (the People's Commissariat for Internal Affairs) and the GPU (the State Political Directorate). The NKVD was supposed to be responsible for the traffic police, firemen and border security but it also managed the Gulag labour camps, suppressed resistance and managed mass deportations. The NKVD was occasionally tasked with organising political assassinations and influencing foreign governments as well. In 1934 it was rebranded as the Soviet Union's National Security Force but its reign of terror continued to mirror the Cheka and tens

SOVIET MILITARY INTELLIGENCE

of thousands of non-conformists were executed or sent to the Gulags during the purges.

The GPU was supposed to gather domestic and foreign intelligence and was initially seen as less brutal than its counterpart because its agents weren't allowed to shoot suspects on sight and had to bring them to trial. Its former leader, Bolshevik party member Mikhail Trilisser, was himself executed by Stalin's forces in 1940. By 1934, the GPU had morphed into the GUGB, a Main Directorate for State Security. Immediately after the Second World War, this organisation became the NKGB, the People's Commissariat for State Security, which then evolved into the MGB, the Ministry for State Security. When this merged with the MVD (the Ministry for Internal

ABOVE The Lubyanka Building was formerly the headquarters of the KGB

SOVIET MILITARY INTELLIGENCE

Affairs), the result was the KGB.

According to *Time* Magazine, the KGB was soon the world's premier intelligence-gathering organisation. Its modus operandi involved secreting officers into countries legally but then having them procure information illegally. As they were usually based at

SOVIET MILITARY INTELLIGENCE

the Soviet Embassy or Consulate, they were protected by diplomatic immunity. Officers who were compromised were usually expelled from the country and returned to the Soviet Union. The alternative was to become an illegal alien who wasn't protected by the state and who worked independently to penetrate foreign organisations before reporting back to the Soviet Union.

During the Cold War, the KGB became particularly adept at gathering political, economic and military intelligence in the USA. Their officers stole documents, codenames and military secrets, as well as infiltrating the CIA and FBI to influence policy and plan assassinations. They scored notable successes in gathering technological intelligence about rocket propulsion and data encryption, as well as infiltrating the Manhattan Project and Los Alamos Laboratory.

The agency also kept close tabs on the Soviet Union's satellite states. As such, the KGB played a key role in quelling the 1956 Hungarian Revolution and the bid for democracy by Czechoslovakia in 1968. The KGB combated ideological subversion at home and arrested hundreds of dissidents who were pushing for democracy over communism. The organisation already had moles in the United States so it then tried to buy three Californian banks to gain access to industrial secrets. The CIA blocked the transaction, however.

The two organisations also came to blows in Bangladesh when the KGB tried to install communist sympathiser Sheikh Mujibur Rahman. The CIA countered by funding Mohammad Mohammadullah's Bangladesh Awami League Party. Rahman won the election but was assassinated in 1975. For the next six years the Americans and Russians would fight over who should govern Bangladesh. The KGB was also involved in the invasion of Afghanistan, and it helped the country's Communist Party organise a coup against the Shah.

When Mikhail Gorbachev came to power in 1985, he'd set about reforming the Soviet Union's political and economic landscape and tried to introduce a policy of openness towards Europe and the West. This angered traditionalists and caused some of the satellite states to question their place within the establishment. As the economy spiralled out of control, Estonia, Latvia, Lithuania and Georgia declared their independence from the Soviet Union. Russia de-

LEFT An aerial view of the Los Alamos complex. The KGB infiltrated the Manhattan Project at this site at the end of the Second World War

SOVIET MILITARY INTELLIGENCE

clared its sovereignty over the states and it appeared as if the Soviet Union would become a federation of independent republics with a common president and army.

KGB Chairman Vladimir Kryuchkov realised the union was under threat and drew up a plan to oust Gorbachev in December 1990. He'd already placed Gorbachev under surveillance so he knew that the prime minister had begun recruiting allies like Boris Yeltsin and Kazakh President Nursultan Nazarbayev should the unthinkable happen.

Gorbachev went on holiday in August 1991 so Kryuchkov made his move in a desperate attempt to safeguard the union. He dispatched Oleg Baklanov from the Defence Council, Oleg Shenin from the Central Committee, and Defence Minister Valentin Varennikov to the Crimea to confront Gorbachev and insist that he either declare a state of emergency or resign in favour of Vice-President Gennady Yanayev (who was also in on the conspiracy). Gorbachev refused so the KGB severed his communications and placed him under armed guard. Kryuchkov then recalled all KGB personnel who were on leave and doubled their pay in preparation for

SOVIET MILITARY INTELLIGENCE

Yanayev's accession to power. Yanayev then signed a declaration allowing him to manage the situation as acting president while Gorbachev recovered from an apparent illness.

Only newspapers and television stations controlled by the State Committee on the State of Emergency (GKChP) were allowed to broadcast. Armoured units under their command then rumbled into Moscow but the conspirators made a crucial error by failing to arrest Yeltsin. On August 19, 1991 Yeltsin announced from the parliament building that a coup was taking place so the conspirators decided to silence him by attacking the building. The route to parliament was blocked by civilians so the conspirators decided not to risk confronting them and withdrew their troops. Gorbachev then returned to Moscow and rounded them all up. The satellite states took their cue and began declaring independence from the end of the month. The GKChP members were all charged with treason but all were eventually offered amnesty.

The KGB was dissolved in the immediate aftermath. Today, its functions have been absorbed by the Foreign Intelligence Service (SVR), the Federal

Mikhail Gorbachev's policies allowed Soviet relations with the West to warm and brought about the end of the Cold War

SOVIET MILITARY INTELLIGENCE

Security Service (FSB) and the Main Intelligence Directorate (GRU). The GRU was initially backed by Leon Trotsky and the Red Army and was tasked with handling military intelligence from sources outside the Soviet Union. Its first director was formerly with the Cheka, Janis Berzin, a Latvian communist who was eventually executed by Stalin in 1937.

The GRU may have existed alongside the NKVD and GPU but the organisations were fierce rivals rather than allies and their agents infiltrated one another to gather intelligence on the state of Soviet security. When the KGB was dissolved for its involvement in the 1991 coup, the GRU remained as the country's most influential intelligence agency. Indeed it can be compared with both the CIA and FBI as it performs many of the same functions as its American counterparts.

At its peak, the GRU employed 350,000 officers and had departments gathering human intelligence, signals intelligence, as well as space and imagery intelligence, particularly in and around the US, where it is rumoured they have stashed several compact nuclear RA-115 'suitcase' bombs. Stanislav Lunev apparently confirmed these allegations when he became the highest-ranking GRU officer to defect to the US in 1992. He also suggested that caches of biological and chemical weapons would be used to poison public drinking water in the US if relations between them cooled to the point of war.

The current head of the GRU is Igor Sergun. He is the highest-ranking intelligence officer in Russia so he reports directly to President Vladimir Putin. Putin was a KGB officer for 16 years before he moved into politics and joined Boris Yeltsin's administration in 1996.

BELOW Igor Sergun is the latest head of Russian Military Intelligence

Chapter 13
Doctor Humam Khalil Al-Balawi

Humam Khalil Al-Balawi was born in Kuwait in 1977 but the family was forced to flee the country to Jordan after the Iraqi invasion in 1990. He studied medicine at Istanbul University and married a Turkish journalist. He was known to support violent extremism and wrote blogs for extremist Islamist websites.

He was brought in by the Jordanian security services in 2007 in the hope that they could transform him into a double agent loyal to the US and Jordan. The CIA and Jordanian intelligence soon viewed him as a trusted source. Although neither organisation claimed to have recruited him for fieldwork, he was supposed to infiltrate Al Qaeda in Pakistan's tribal

LEFT Humam Khalil Abu-Mulal Al-Balawi

DOCTOR HUMAM KHALIL AL-BALAWI

areas along the Afghan border.

Al-Balawi was taken to an American forward operating base, Camp Chapman, in Afghanistan in 2009 after he claimed to have information about Al Qaeda's Ayman Al-Zawahiri, the current leader of the organisation and a man with a $25-million price on his head. Al-Balawi was then collected by the external chief of security and driven through three of the camp's checkpoints without being stopped.

When the car pulled over near the building where Al-Balawi was to be debriefed, he climbed out and detonated a bomb sewn into a suicide vest. Seven CIA officers (including the head of the base), a Jordanian intelligence officer, the Afghan driver and Al-Balawi were killed, and another six CIA personnel were seriously injured. It was the worst loss of life for the agency in a single attack since the US Embassy in Beirut was bombed in 1983, which left eight dead.

BELOW Jennifer Lynne Matthews was the base commander at Camp Chapman. She was killed in the suicide attack

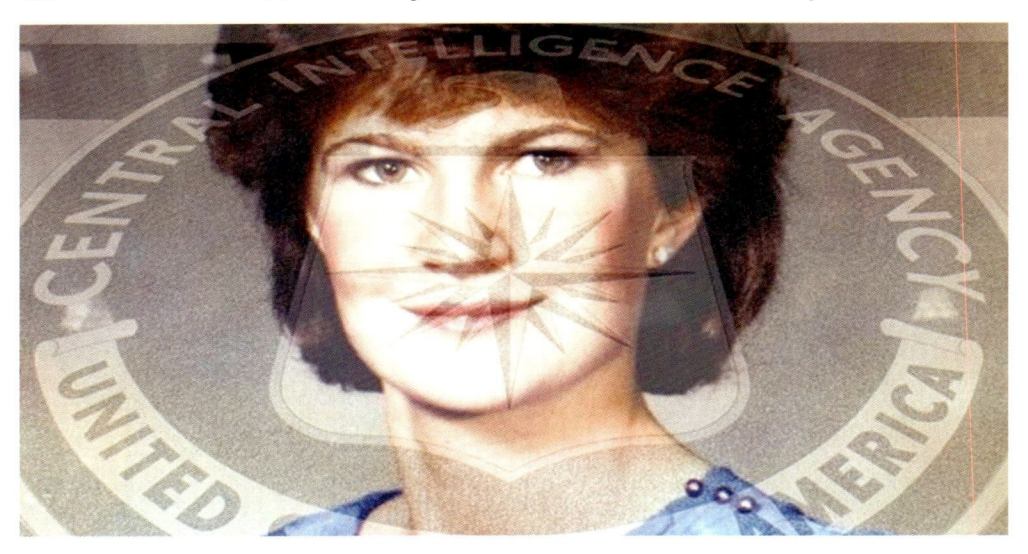

Chapter 14

Nathan Hale

Nathan Hale was born in Connecticut in 1755 and he went to Yale College at the age of 14. He was a bright student who excelled in maths, astronomy and literature, and he graduated in 1773. He began working as a teacher but joined the Connecticut militia at the outbreak of the Revolutionary War.

He wasn't sure about fighting on the frontline but an old classmate, Ben Tallmadge, wrote to him and convinced him to accept a commission in the 7th Connecticut Regiment. Their first assignment was to protect New York from the British but, as the location of the invasion of Manhattan Island couldn't be determined, General Washington

BELOW Rendition of the Beekman House

NATHAN HALE

tried to recruit spies to infiltrate the British ranks. Hale was the only volunteer.

Immediately before he left for the city, the British captured Long Island. On September 12, 1776, Hale was ferried across the river. Three days later, the southern tip of Manhattan Island also fell to the British and General Washington was pushed north into what is now Morningside Heights. Much of lower Manhattan was then razed to the ground in the Great New York Fire, which may have been started by the British or possibly American saboteurs trying to keep the city out of their hands.

Hale had barely passed any useful information back to Washington when he was spotted and recognised in a tavern near Flushing Bay by Major Robert Rogers of the Queen's Rangers. He took Hale aside and confided that he was also an American patriot, tricking Hale into exposing himself. He took the captured spy to General William Howe's headquarters at the Beekman House in rural Manhattan, and an interrogation and search revealed Hale was carrying physical evidence relating to British troop movements.

Hale was held overnight at the house before being marched down Post Road to the Dove Tavern on the morning of September 22. Before he was hanged, he is said to have given a speech that included the line: "I am so satisfied with the cause in which I have engaged that my only regret is that I have not more lives than one to offer in its service."

BELOW The British hang Nathan Hale in 1776

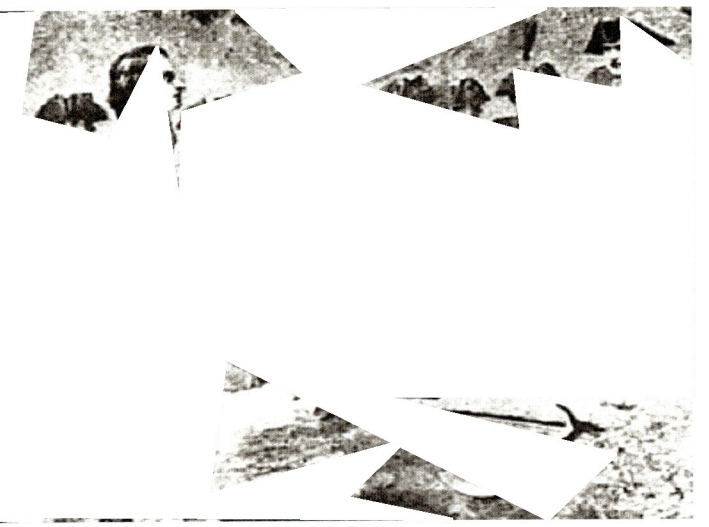

Chapter 15

Virginia Hall

Virginia Hall was born in Baltimore in 1906. She had a privileged upbringing and studied languages at Columbia University before travelling to Europe to apply the finishing touches to her education. She soon landed a job as a clerk in the American Embassy in Warsaw but her hopes of working in the Foreign Service were dashed when she accidentally shot herself in the leg while on a hunting trip in Turkey. The leg had to be amputated so she resigned from the State Department in 1939.

By the outbreak of the Second World War she was in Paris. She joined the medical services and moved to the Vichy territory when the French surrendered in 1940. She then went to London to join Britain's Special Operations Executive before returning to France to work for the Resistance. She escaped to Madrid when the rest of France fell in 1942 but returned once more to France to map drop zones and coordinate raids by the Resistance. She was high on the Gestapo's most-wanted list but she continued providing the Allies with information until after the Normandy Landings.

After the war, she married fellow agent Paul Goillot and joined the CIA as an intelligence analyst. General William Donovan then awarded her the Distinguished Service Cross, the only one presented to a female civilian for work undertaken during the conflict. President Truman wanted to give her a public ceremony but Hall valued her anonymity and was still working undercover. She died in 1982 in Maryland close to where she was born.

VIRGINIA HALL

General William Donovan presents Virginia Hall with a Distinguished Service Cross

Chapter 16

Mata Hari

Margaretha Geertruida Zelle was born in the Netherlands in August 1876. Her father was a successful businessman and she enjoyed a privileged childhood, but he then lost his money after a series of poor investments. This led to her parents divorcing, and her mother died in 1891. Her father remarried but Zelle moved in with her godfather and trained to become a teacher. The headmaster ended up flirting with her so her godfather suggested she move to her uncle's house in The Hague.

In 1894 she answered an advert placed by an aristocratic Captain Rudolf MacLeod stating that he wished to find a wife. The couple married the following year and she suddenly found herself moving in high society. They moved to Java and had two children but MacLeod turned out to be an abusive alcoholic so she left him and embarked on a career as a dancer with the stage name Mata Hari. Both children died – probably from complications due to syphilis – so she went to Paris and joined a circus.

She continued her dancing, and her provocative stage act was an instant hit. She singlehandedly revolutionised the exotic dance show and established a fascination with the human body that would become famous in Paris. So many imitators joined the circuit, however, that her career gradually declined and she performed her last show in 1915. She maintained relationships with countless military officials and politicians and, as war approached, she was seen more of a

MATA HARI

seductress rather than a free-spirited artist.

The Netherlands remained neutral during the war so she was able to visit Spain, Britain and France, but she soon came to the attention of British Intelligence and was arrested at Falmouth in 1916. She was questioned by Sir Basil Thomson and eventually admitted to working for the French government, although her story has never been corroborated.

In December, the French War Ministry deliberately allowed her to overhear the names of six Belgian agents, one of whom was suspected of working as a double agent for Germany and the French. Mata Hari travelled to Madrid and, two weeks later, the double agent was executed by the Germans, satisfying the French that she must have transmitted this information to them.

Early the following year, the British intercepted a German message from Madrid to Berlin that referred to a useful spy with the codename H-21. The French knew that the message referred to Mata Hari so she was arrested in Paris and put on trial

MATA HARI

in July 1917. She vehemently protested her innocence but her trial was anything but fair so she was convicted of betraying 50,000 soldiers and executed by firing squad in October at the age of 41.

When the Germans released their documents relating to the case in 1970 it emerged that Mata Hari had joined the German war effort under Captain Hoffman in 1915. There seems to be little doubt that she used her sexuality to extract information from French officers before betraying them to the Germans. No one claimed her body after her death and it eventually disappeared from the Museum of Anatomy in Paris.

LEFT Mata Hari's arrest photo

BELOW Mata Hari's scrapbook chronicling her wartime exploits

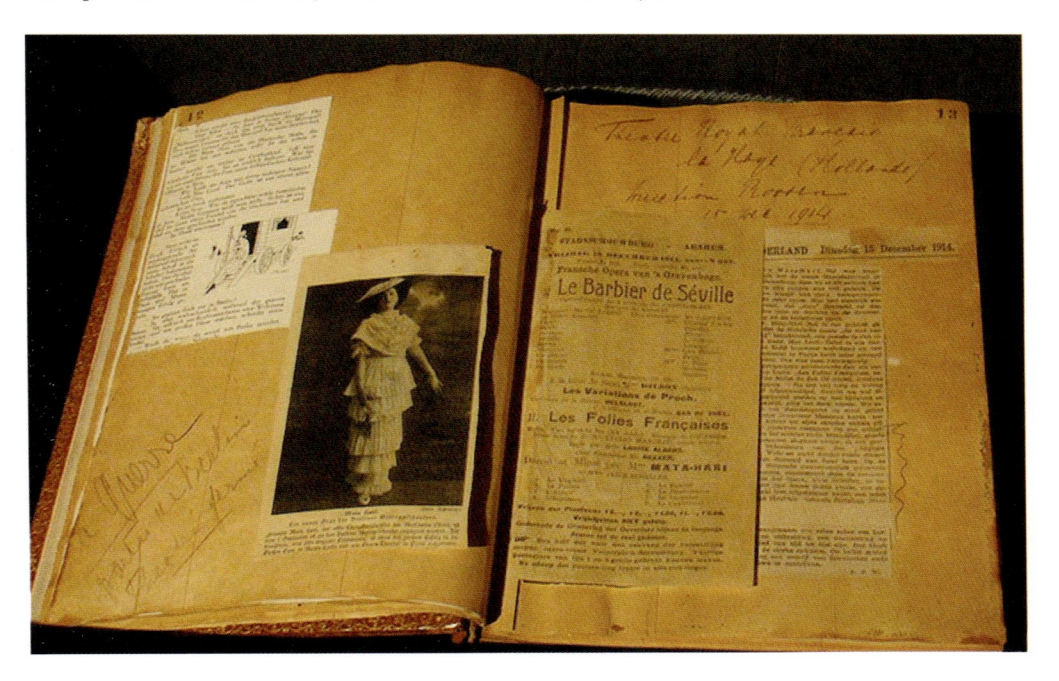

Alexander Litvinenko

Alexander Litvinenko was born in Voronezh in the Soviet Union in 1962. He joined the Ministry of Internal Affairs in 1980 but continued studying for the next five years and eventually graduated as a platoon commander. By 1986 he'd been recruited by the KGB as an informer for military counter-intelligence. He served as an operational officer for the next five years before being promoted to Federal Counterintelligence. He worked mainly in counter-terrorism and organised crime but also saw active service in Chechnya.

He met Russian oligarch Boris Berezovsky in 1994 and worked part-time on his security detail to make up for his low state salary. Although this was illegal, the FSB overlooked his secondary career and soon promoted him to senior operational officer, although contemporaries view the FSB's work undermining organised crime something of a conflict of interest: how can you in-

ALEXANDER LITVINENKO

vestigate crime impartially when you're one of the people involved?

Litvinenko soon realised that many Russian officials and politicians had links with criminal groups so he came to the conclusion that the entire system was corrupt. In December 1997, the FSB ordered him to kill Berezovsky but he refused. The following year, Litvinenko and four more FSB officers, all of whom also worked for Berezovsky and the Directorate of Analysis and Suppression of Criminal Groups, stated at a press conference that the directorate had indeed ordered them to kill their secondary employer.

Litvinenko was arrested on Putin's orders and fired from the FSB but he defied an order not to leave the country and travelled to Turkey. The Americans denied his request for asylum but the British accepted him, although they claimed this was on humanitarian grounds rather than to extract information from him. He became a journalist and joined Berezovsky's campaign to discredit Putin's government.

Litvinenko was most likely recruited by MI6 as a low-level informant and consultant in 2003. This brought him back to the attention of the FSB, and former officer Mikhail Trepashkin warned Litvinenko that a unit had been tasked with killing him. Litvinenko didn't take the threat seriously and even began making unsubstantiated claims about the power structure in Moscow. He alleged, for example, that the Kremlin was behind or was forewarned about the shooting in the Armenian Parliament and the Russian apartment block bombings in 1999, the Moscow theatre hostage crisis in 2002, and the Beslan school terrorist attack, as well as having links with terrorist organisations like Al Qaeda.

Litvinenko was suddenly taken ill in November 2006. The hospital revealed he had been poisoned with radioactive polonium-210 and he died 23 days later. Before his death, Litvinenko revealed that he had met former KGB agents Dmitri Kovtun and Andrei Lugovoi early on the day he fell ill. A leaked American diplomatic cable revealed that Kovtun had left traces of polonium in a house and car he had been using, and Lugovoi failed a question on a lie-detector test about whether he had ever handled polonium.

Litvinenko and his family suggested his green tea had been laced with the

LEFT Alexander Litvinenko

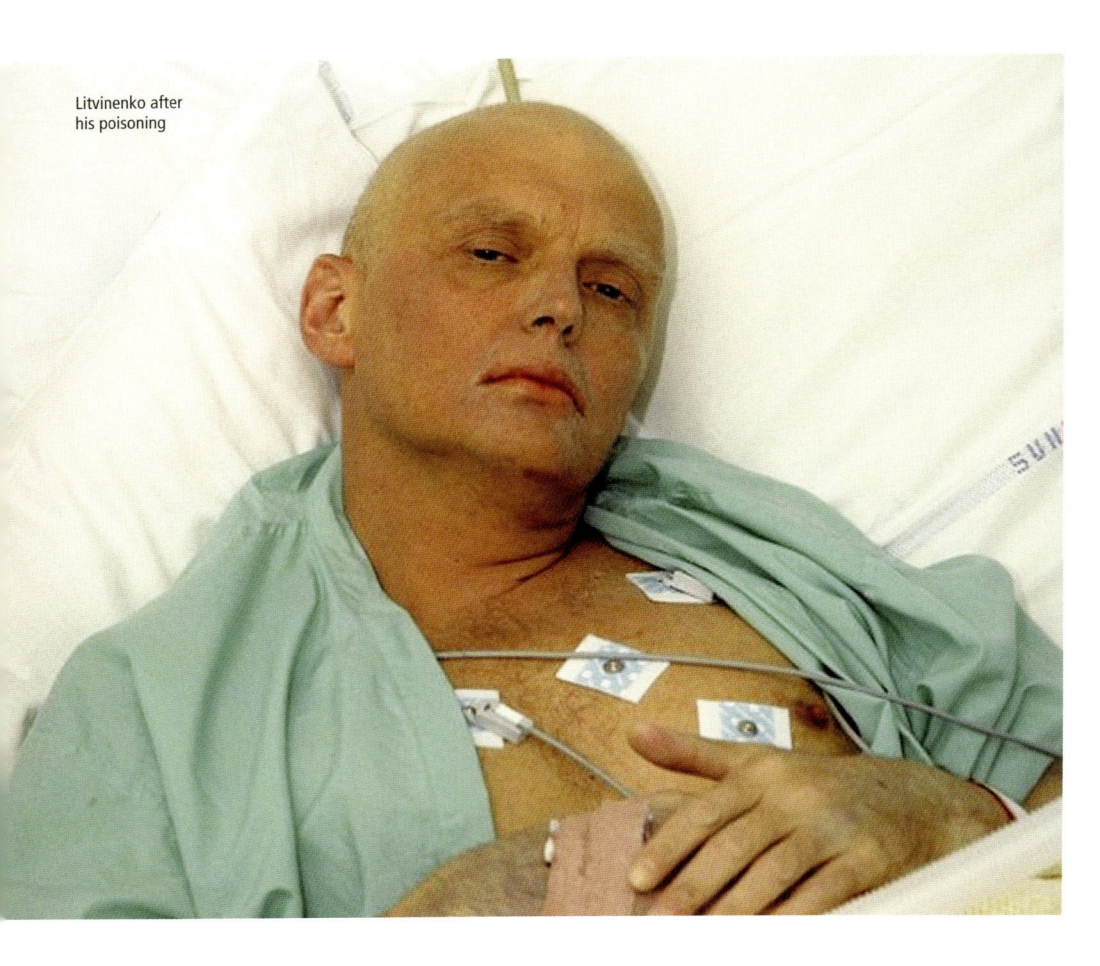

ALEXANDER LITVINENKO

Litvinenko after his poisoning

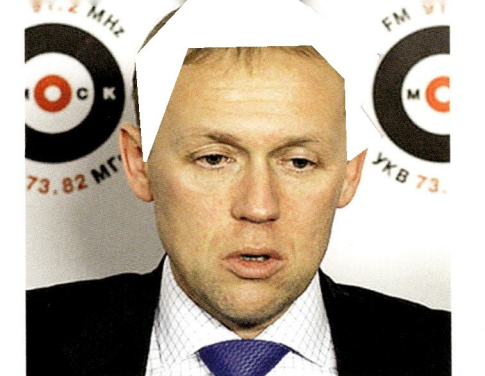

ALEXANDER LITVINENKO

radioactive material and laid the blame squarely on the Putin regime, but the Kremlin categorically denied any involvement and Kovtun claimed to the British inquiry that Litvinenko might have poisoned himself accidentally.

LEFT Andrei Lugovoi

BELOW Dimitri Kovtun

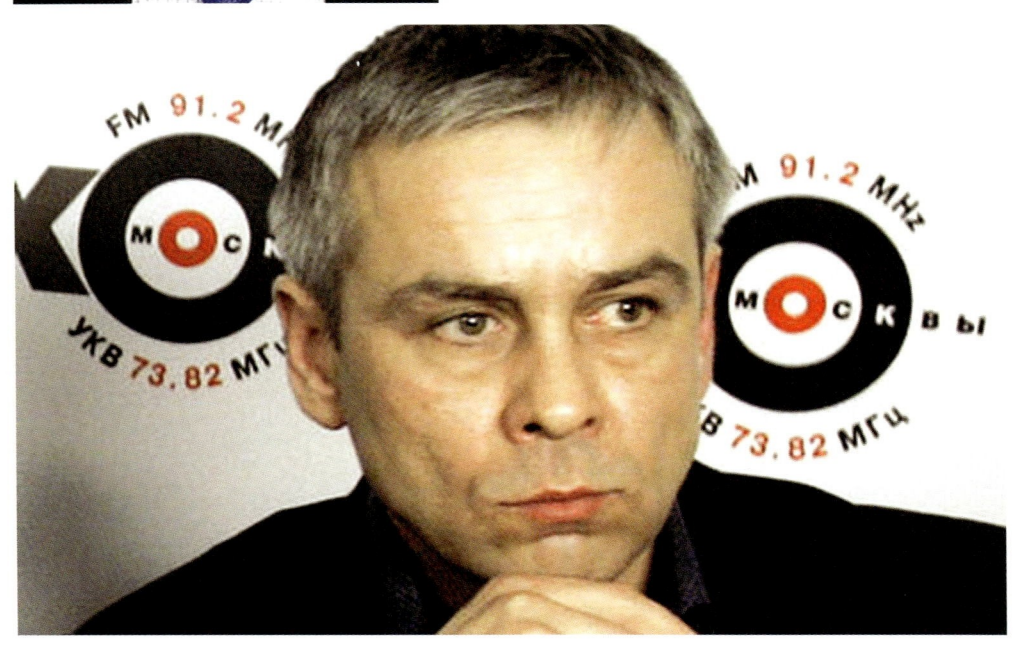

Chapter 18

MI5 and MI6

MI5 (Military Intelligence, Section 5) is Britain's domestic security service. MI6 performs many of the same counterintelligence duties but is more concerned with foreign operations. Both were borne out of the Secret Service Bureau that was formed by members of the Admiralty and the War Office in 1909 to combat Imperial German pretensions in Europe.

The admiralty was primarily concerned with monitoring the German navy, so its operations were conducted in the naval yards of northern Germany. The army, meanwhile, was tasked with domestic counterintelligence and the capture of enemy spies inside the UK. This latter agency evolved into the Directorate of Military Intelligence, Section 5, the name by which it is still known, albeit unofficially, today (it is now simply the Security Service).

The first Head of Domestic Intelligence was Major-General Sir Vernon Kell, who became known within the agency as 'K'. He oversaw the operation to identify German spies in Britain during the war but the Metropolitan Police's Special Branch was then responsible for their arrest. Within 24 hours of war being declared, Home Secretary Reginald McKenna claimed that 22 spies had been apprehended, although most were already known to the security services. When he researched the story in 2006, journalist Nicholas Hiley believed the spies were actually arrested much later and the initial claim was pure propaganda.

Most of the German agents who en-

MI5 AND MI6

Sir Vernon Kell was the first head of MI5

MI5 AND MI6

tered Britain were identified by MI5 officers monitoring the entry and exit points as well as by opening mail. After the war, the attention shifted to the Soviet Union as their spies were trying to drum up support for communism within the UK. As Britain was sending officers into Russia to help overthrow the government in the aftermath of the revolution, both sides were actively engaged in espionage throughout the 1920s. MI5 was also tasked with monitoring British citizens who might have been influenced by communist ideology.

However, the agency then saw its budget cut by 70% and its staff reduced from 800 to just 12 so it was unable to compete with the rise of Special Branch and ended up without a clear goal during the Irish War of Independence. In fact the agency was reduced to helping train army case officers, although most were compromised by Michael Collins's counterintelligence unit on Bloody Sunday in 1920. The British responded by shooting dead 14 civilians during a Gaelic Football match at Croke Park.

The intelligence failings in the province forced Prime Minister David Lloyd George to revoke the powers

MI5 AND MI6

of the Home Intelligence Directorate and transfer it back to Kell's MI5. The agency then had the rather dubious distinction of helping Benito Mussolini enter politics in Italy. They promised him a weekly wage of £100 (more than £6,000 today) if he alienated anti-war protesters and published pro-war propaganda in the hope that Italy would help defeat Germany. Two years later, Mussolini reformed the Fascist Party and by 1922 he was the youngest prime minster in Italian history.

MI5's woes continued into the 1930s when it became apparent that its methods of intelligence gathering were outdated. While Kell was relying on agents infiltrating organisations and bribing officials to learn more about them, the Soviet NKVD was recruiting members of the British establishment, some of whom, such as the Cambridge Five, already worked for the security services.

Kim Philby and his cohorts passed sensitive information to the Soviets for the duration of the war, but MI5 was also unprepared for the influx of enemy agents during the conflict. Winston Churchill realised Kell was no longer the right man for the job so he replaced him with SIS operative David Petrie.

With the German failure during the Battle of Britain in 1940, the number of enemy agents coming to Britain to prepare for the Nazi invasion fell abruptly. This allowed Petrie to concentrate on turning the agents already captured rather than imprisoning them under Colonel Robin 'Tin Eye' Stephens at Latchmere House and then executing them. And so began Operation Double-Cross, an elaborate system of feeding the Germans disinformation from supposedly reliable agents in Britain. It was a hugely successful operation, particularly in the build-up to D-Day when the Germans were convinced the main attack would occur in the Pas de Calais.

The suspicion surrounding the Soviet Union in the post-war period was brought home when Philby's Cambridge spy ring was eventually exposed. The KGB penetrated both British Intelligence and the CIA, as well as the Tube Alloys and Manhattan Projects (Britain and America's atomic bomb development respectively). Although these high-profile intelligence failures were those that made the headlines, the agencies'

MI5 AND MI6

MI5 AND MI6

successes were rarely reported for obvious reasons. This is why we tend to hear about spies who were only caught after years of betraying their countries, and why the security services come under fire for not protecting the public from terrorist attacks like those that happened in London in 2005. We hardly ever hear about terrorist plots that are foiled and, even if we do, the details of how the security services came by their information and were able to act remain shrouded in secrecy.

MI5 did break another Soviet spy network and expelled 105 embassy staff in 1971, but it then emerged that the agency kept files on many politicians, trade unions and prominent celebrities. When Jack Straw became Home Secretary in 1997, he discovered MI5 had a file on him from his days as a student radical.

As relations with Mikhail Gorbachev and the Soviet bloc warmed towards the end of the 1980s, MI5 diverted its resources to monitoring activity in Northern Ireland. It also supported loyalist paramilitary groups during the troubles, for which David Cameron apologised in 2012. Today, MI5 is tasked with working alongside the National Crime Agency to prevent domestic terrorism, combat organised crime, protect British political and economic interests, and ensure internal security.

MI6 began life as a foreign intelligence service concerned with counter-espionage. It was formed in 1909 but came to prominence during the First World War when Britain sent officers to Germany to report on the strength and capability of the Imperial Navy.

Whereas MI5 had Vernon Kell as 'K' as its first chief, the Secret Intelligence Service had Captain Sir George Mansfield Smith-Cumming, who went by the codename 'C'. Although Cumming sent officers into Germany to spy on the fleet, they were only able to establish intelligence networks in the countries bordering Germany and their effectiveness was limited.

The SIS budget was also cut in the aftermath of the conflict but Cumming managed to ensure it returned to Foreign Office control and insisted that its officers had diplomatic immunity. With Germany forced to pay extortionate reparations between the wars, the SIS turned its attention to the Soviet Union and even dispatched Sidney Reilly to help overthrow the Bolshevik govern-

RIGHT Kim Philby was perhaps the biggest embarrassment to British Intelligence

MI5 AND MI6

ment. He was caught and executed for his part in the conspiracy.

When Cumming died in 1923, he was succeeded by Sir Hugh Sinclair. The new 'C' introduced Section V to monitor foreign counterintelligence, as well as economic departments, a signals organisation, and a covert paramilitary wing that would become the Special Operations Executive in the Second World War. In the 1930s, the rise of Nazism saw the agency shift its focus back to Germany. As well as gathering intelligence directly using officers on the ground, more emphasis was placed on cracking German codes, feeding the enemy disinformation, and analysing reconnaissance imagery.

The first directive was handled by the cryptanalysis team under Alan Turing at Bletchley Park, and it was his primitive computer, the electromagnetic Bombe (not Colossus), that finally cracked the German Enigma Code. This gave the Allies an enormous technological advantage and probably shortened the war by two years, saving as many as five million lives.

Working in tandem with MI5, the SIS programme of feeding the Germans misleading information was also

MI5 AND MI6

extremely successful. They convinced the German High Command that the D-Day attack would actually occur in the Pas de Calais under the codename Operation Fortitude, for example. An equally elaborate deception codenamed Operation Mincemeat convinced the Germans in the Mediterranean that the Allies were heading for Sardinia and Greece when their real target was Sicily.

The latter deception involved planting fake documents on a body and allowing it to wash up on the Spanish coast after an apparent air crash. The Spanish authorities were known to hand over sensitive information to the Abwehr so the documents would soon find themselves in German hands. The documents included a complete fake identity plus letters from the British to the Americans discussing Operation Husky, the planned invasion of Greece.

The British delivered the body by submarine and it was found by a local fisherman the following morning. The Spanish promptly alerted Adolf Clauss and the Germans held the body for three days before returning it to the British for burial. His obituary then appeared in the *Times* to complete the façade. The Germans made copies of all the documents and sent the transcripts back to Berlin, all of which was detected by the code-breakers at Bletchley Park.

Joseph Goebbels and Benito Mussolini remained sceptical about the body and the implications of the documents, but Hitler swallowed the ruse and redeployed infantry and armoured divisions from Sicily to Greece, Sardinia and Corsica. He then sent Erwin Rommel to Greece to assume command of the German defence of southern Europe. On July 9, 1943, the Allies attacked Sicily but Hitler refused to send reinforcements for two weeks because he believed this to be a feint rather than the main assault. It was a catastrophic error of judgement that proved the vital role disinformation from the SIS had in determining the outcome of the war. To compound their misery, when the Germans discovered genuine documents on an abandoned landing craft about legitimate targets on D-Day, they were ignored as another deception as Hitler believed the main thrust would come through the Pas de Calais.

However, the service also had to cope with its share of intelligence failures: two SIS officers were abducted by the SS in Venlo in the Netherlands, and Kim Phil-

LEFT Sir Mansfield Cumming was the first head of MI6 and was known as 'C'

MI5 AND MI6

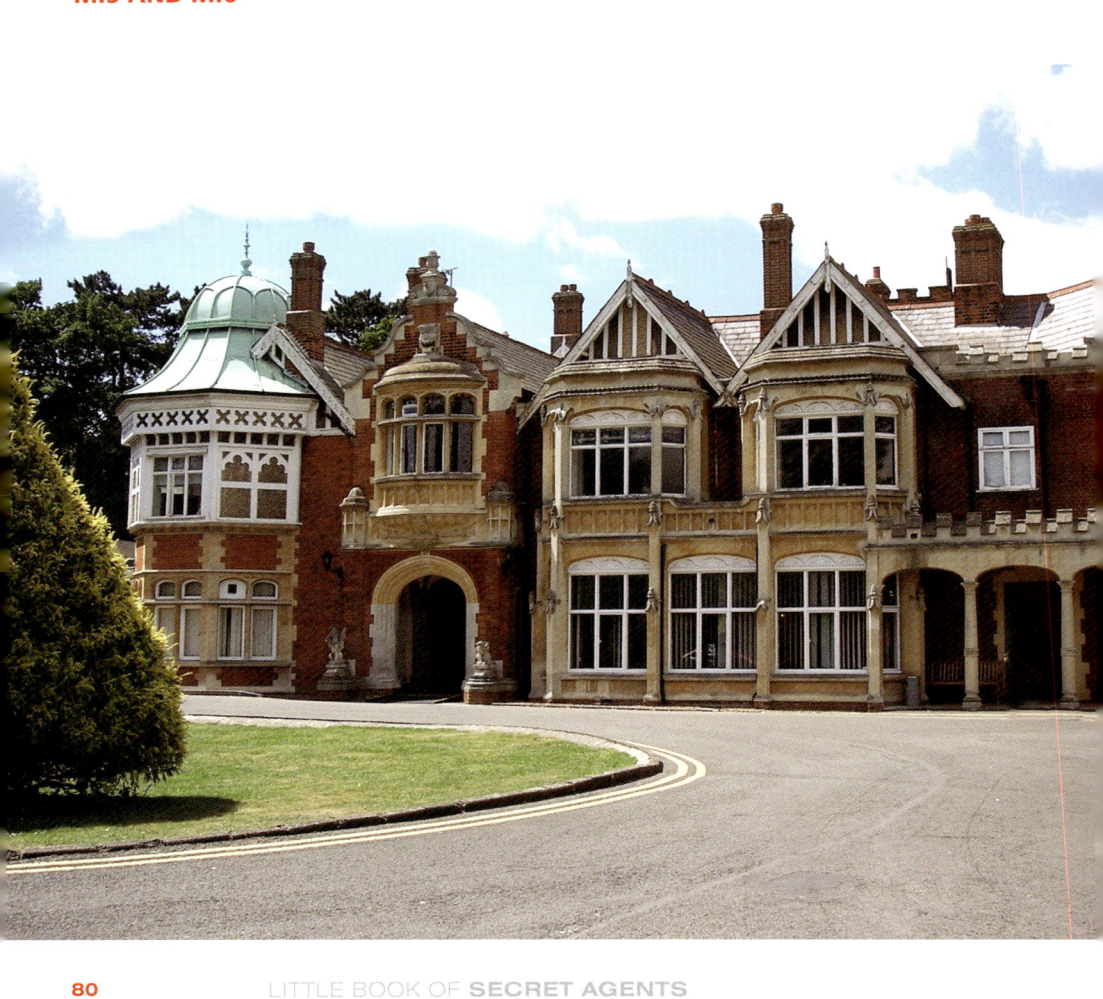

MI5 AND MI6

OPPOSITE Bletchley Park today

LEFT Alan Turing was the mathematical genius who built one of the first supercomputers

MI5 AND MI6

by's Cambridge spy ring haemorrhaged sensitive information to the Soviet Union throughout the war and into the Cold War. When his conspirators defected in the early 1950s, Philby was forced to retire from the intelligence service. SIS operations in Vienna and Berlin were also compromised by double agents.

The SIS and CIA helped overthrow Mohammad Mosaddegh in Iran in 1953, and they also infiltrated the Polish Ministry of Public Security, delivering information to both agencies for which the Americans agreed to pay $20 million. The SIS also enjoyed considerable success planting its officers within the GRU, and both Oleg Penkovsky and Oleg Gordievsky proved invaluable assets during the Cuban Missile Crisis and throughout the 1970s. In 1982, KGB officer Vladimir Kuzichkin defected to the West and was able to provide details about the organisation's plans to overthrow Gorbachev in the August Coup of 1991. The coup was ultimately unsuccessful and the KGB was gradually disbanded afterwards.

As threats from elsewhere in the world became the priority, the SIS was restructured under Sir Colin McColl to deal with counter-proliferation, counter-terrorism, counter-narcotics and organised crime, and a new global issues section was established. It was also McColl's policy to open up the agency to scrutiny by Parliament's Intelligence and Security Committee. The SIS then moved into its new headquarters at Vauxhall Cross on the Albert Embankment overlooking Vauxhall Bridge. (It had previously been based at 54, Broadway between 1924 and 1966, and at 100, Westminster Bridge Road in Lambeth from 1966 until 1995.)

The distinctive new building was designed by Sir Terry Farrell and incorporates blast-protection technology, back-up power generators and shielding from electronic eavesdropping. It was attacked in two James Bond films (*The World Is Not Enough* and *Skyfall*) and once in reality by the IRA in 2000. They fired a Russian-built anti-tank rocket that struck the eighth floor but the explosion only caused superficial damage.

Cuts to the defence budget led to several departments merging in the late 1990s and this created confusion about whether Saddam Hussein did possess weapons of mass destruction, and whether Colonel Gaddafi and other African leaders posed a threat to

LEFT A replica of Turing's Bombe computer that helped crack the Enigma Code

MI5 AND MI6

RIGHT The headquarters of the Secret Intelligence Service at Vauxhall Cross in London

the UK's national security. Intelligence about WMD was then allegedly fabricated by the SIS to give Britain and its allies a reason to invade Iraq and remove Saddam from power. When no weapons were found, the SIS came under scrutiny for its perceived failings. It was then criticised for accepting information obtained when the CIA tortured the terror suspects at Guantanamo Bay who were thought to be behind the attack on the USS *Cole* and the World Trade Centres on 9/11. The SIS helped rebuild its reputation when it provided the intelligence that led to the capture of Colonel Gadaffi. The former Libyan leader made two phone calls to his family to say that he was safe but an Anglo-French surveillance operation intercepted the calls, pinpointed his location and sent in the Libyan security services to make the arrest.

Today, the service maintains important overseas stations in Afghanistan and Pakistan as Britain continues the fight against global terrorism. There are also officers reportedly operating in Nigeria and Syria as the world unites against the atrocities committed by terror cells like Boko Haram and Islamic State. The head of the SIS today is Alex Younger.

MI5 AND MI6

Chapter 19

Mossad

Mossad is Israel's national intelligence agency. It was founded in 1949 on the orders of Prime Minister David Ben-Gurion. He wanted better cooperation between the foreign office, army intelligence and the internal security service, so the new organisation was directly responsible to him. Its motto was originally 'By wise guidance you can wage war' but this was changed to 'With no guidance a nation falls, but there is safety with an abundance of counsellors'.

Operating in Israel and the Middle East, the agency became one of the most important and busy intelligence services in the world. It also developed a wider reputation when its officers learnt that Adolf Eichmann had fled to Argentina from Nazi Germany at the end of the Second World War.

A five-man team led by Shimon Ben Aharon entered the country and placed him under surveillance. Having verified his identity, the team abducted him and escaped back to Israel. Eichmann was then tried for war crimes and executed. Argentina complained to the UN Security Council that the infiltration was illegal and breached the rules by which council was governed. The UN acknowledged that the Mossad agents had acted unlawfully but that Eichmann had to be held to account for his role in the Holocaust. On the advice of the UN, Mossad shelved its plan to kidnap Josef Mengele, the 'Angel of Death' who had condemned thousands to the gas chambers in Auschwitz. Mengele eluded capture

MOSSAD

Israeli Prime Minister David Ben-Gurion founded Mossad in 1949

MOSSAD

and eventually drowned off the Brazilian coast in 1979.

While the British SIS are believed not to have a licence to kill, Mossad officers were responsible for the assassination of Nazi sympathiser Herbert Cukurs in 1965. They also planned and carried out Operation Wrath of God, the mission to track down and kill the terrorists who were responsible for the massacre of 11 Israeli athletes at the 1972 Munich Olympics. The operation against militant group Black September and the Palestine Liberation Organisation was launched by Israeli Prime Minister Golda Meir immediately after the Games but it took 20 years before all the terrorists were brought to 'justice'.

Meir was initially cautious about authorising the mission but, when terrorists loyal to the PLO hijacked a Lufthansa passenger aircraft (Flight 615) and demanded the German police release three of the perpetrators who'd been captured during the hostage crisis in Munich, her resolve hardened. She then asked Mossad to draw up a list of everyone thought to be involved in the massacre and instructed the agency to assassinate the 30 people responsible. Meir insisted on retaining plausible deniability in that their deaths could not be linked to Israeli Special Forces. Over the next 16 years, 22 men were hunted down and killed by Mossad operatives, usually by car bombs or two-man hit teams.

At the beginning of the campaign against the PLO and its allies, Ali Hassan Salameh responded for Black September by planning a missile attack on Meir as she flew into Italy to visit the Pope in 1973. He was also negotiating his escape to the Soviet Union after the attack.

Black September smuggled a batch of Strela 2 missiles from Yugoslavia to Bari and then transported them to Fiumicino Airport in Rome. Salameh then ordered his agents in Thailand to launch a diversionary attack on the Israeli Embassy in Bangkok. While the hostage situation there was being resolved, a phone operator in an apartment block in Rome

LEFT Adolf Eichmann at his trial in 1961

BELOW Adolf Eichman's trial judges (left to right) Benjamin Halevi, Moshe Landau, and Yitzhak Raveh

MOSSAD

reported overhearing a conversation in Arabic about a possible attack on Golda Meir. Mossad's Director-General Zvi Zamir acted quickly but both missile teams were in position as Meir's aircraft approached.

Mossad and the Italian security services became involved in a shootout with the occupants of a van parked in a field on the flight-path. The driver escaped on foot but was eventually captured and, after a severe interrogation, he revealed the location of the second unit. The security teams quickly found the second van and rammed it with their truck, trapping the terrorists inside. They were taken to hospital and were eventually allowed to fly to Libya so that the Italians weren't seen as allowing the assassinations to happen on their soil. As soon as the terrorists landed, Mossad agents were waiting for them and finished the job.

The only man who managed to elude

BELOW A Black September terrorist holds Israeli athletes hostage at the 1972 Munich Olympics

them was Salameh, nicknamed the Red Prince and the supposed mastermind behind the massacre. (Black September have since admitted that he was responsible for several terrorist attacks but Munich wasn't one of them.) Mossad agents believed he'd escaped to Lillehammer in Norway but the six officers who travelled to the town wrongly identified Moroccan waiter Ahmed Bouchiki as Salameh and killed an innocent man. Local police arrested and imprisoned six Mossad assassins, although several more eluded the authorities and returned to Israel.

In January 1974, Swiss informants announced that Salameh was scheduled to meet PLO leaders in a church. Two assassins entered the building and killed three men but Salameh wasn't one of them. Mossad then sent agents to London but when their source failed to show for a meeting, they began to suspect they were under surveillance. A female assassin then killed one of the agents after seducing him in a hotel room. The remaining members of the team followed her to Amsterdam and avenged the murder but who had hired her was still a mystery. The commander of Operation Wrath of God, Michael Harari then ordered the hunt for Salameh to be called off, but his team of assassins ignored him and travelled to Spain to follow a lead. A security guard confronted them at a house in Tarifa so he was shot, but the team then aborted an assault on the residence. After so many high-profile failures, Golda Meir ordered the operation be cancelled. It wasn't until Menachem Begin came to power that Mossad was again tasked with bringing Salameh to justice.

He was traced to Beirut in 1978 so Mossad dispatched Erika Chambers to Lebanon. She rented an apartment close to where he'd been seen and arranged for a Volkswagen to be packed with explosives and parked further down the street. When Salameh and his bodyguards drove past, she and her team detonated the bomb, killing Salameh and his security detail. However, four innocent bystanders were also killed and another 18 were seriously injured. Chambers and her team escaped without trace. Yasser Arafat was one of 100,000 people who took to the streets to mourn Salameh's death.

Today, Mossad remains active all over the world. The agency collects intelligence, mounts covert operations, and protects Jewish communities wherever they are threatened.

MOSSAD

Golda Meir initiated Operation Wrath of God to bring the terrorists to justice

Chapter 20
Melita Norwood

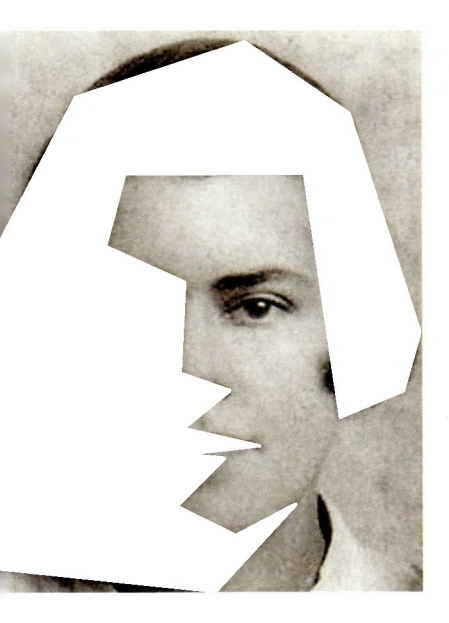

Melita Sirnis was born in Hampshire in 1912 to parents who moved in socialist circles. She married Hilary Norwood, a Russian teacher, in 1935 (the family had changed their name from Nussbaum on arriving in England) and quickly bought into his communist ideals. She was recruited by Soviet Intelligence (the NKVD) in 1937 and provided them with state secrets while working at the British Non-Ferrous Metals Research Association, a company specialising in analytical chemistry, metallurgy, physics and spectrography.

During the war, the company secured vital defence contracts, some of which involved assessing the problems posed by corrosive seawater on ships' hulls or

LEFT Melita Norwood

ABOVE Norwood in 1999

underwater pipes. Norwood was hired as a clerk but was soon promoted to secretary to a research superintendent so she had access to hundreds of classified papers, many of which she passed on to her Soviet handlers. As the company was involved with building Britain's first atomic bomb, she also photographed these top-secret documents.

The Russians valued her work so highly that she was considered more important than the Cambridge Five and was perhaps the most valuable female agent ever recruited by the USSR. After the war, Soviet military intelligence and the KGB competed to handle her, with the KGB coming out on top and mining her for information until her retirement in 1972. They even paid her a monthly pension of £20.

Her activity wasn't revealed to the public until Vasili Mitrokhin, a senior archivist for the Soviet Foreign Intelligence Service, released her file in 1999. He'd defected to the West in 1992 and immediately informed British Intelligence but the information was considered too sensitive to be released immediately. Norwood, who went under the codename Hola, was never prosecuted and died in 2005 at the age of 93.

… Chapter 21

The NSA

The National Security Agency is an American organisation that collects and processes signals information for domestic and foreign intelligence purposes. It also protects government communications and systems from cyber-attack and is authorised to gather intelligence covertly using bugging, electronic sabotage, eavesdropping and satellite surveillance.

The NSA began life as a code-decryption service towards the end of the First World War. This small branch of military intelligence was based in Washington, DC and originally consisted of Director Herbert Yardley and two civilian contractors. At the end of the war, it merged with the navy's cryptanalysis branch and moved to New York as Military Intelligence, Section 8 (MI-8).

The unit grew throughout the 1920s and both the State Department and War Department authorised it to monitor foreign communications by accessing Western Union's wire transfers. This led to mail intercepts and a sharing of information with the British and French. By 1929, however, Secretary of State Henry Stimson had shut the unit down as he believed it breached basic privacy laws: "Gentlemen do not read each other's mail."

The unit evolved into the Signal Security Agency in the Second World War. It worked alongside the British codebreakers at Bletchley Park to intercept and decipher German and Japanese communications. After the war, it was absorbed by the army (ASA) and put

THE NSA

ABOVE The headquarters of the National Security Agency at Fort Meade in Maryland

RIGHT Henry Stimson shut down MI-8 in 1929

under the command of a Director of Military Intelligence. The agency was initially criticised by President Truman because it failed to liaise with the CIA and FBI so it was rebranded as the top-secret NSA in 1952.

The agency was responsible for intercepting communications throughout the Vietnam War, both in the war zone itself and those exchanged between civilians in the United States, including celebrities like Jane Fonda, Martin Luther King and John Lennon. It was also responsible for tapping phones during the Watergate scandal. It then intercepted messages from the Libyan government after the bombing of a nightclub in Berlin. President Ronald Reagan used this 'evidence' as justification for bombing Libya in 1986.

The 9/11 and 7/7 attacks highlighted just how poorly prepared the West was

THE NSA

to deal with large-scale terrorist attacks. Surveillance operations were stepped up as intercepting communications between the terrorists responsible could have given the authorities time to take preventative measures. Programmes such as ThinThread, Trailblazer and Turbulence allowed the NSA to monitor more suspicious transmissions and even implant viruses in enemy computing systems but they were inordinately expensive, required countless staff to manage properly, and didn't always provide decipherable data.

In 2013, former NSA employee Edward Snowden announced that the agency routinely intercepts a billion phone calls and emails. These aren't confined to suspected terrorists as the agency also collects data on politics, economics and industrial espionage from every corner of the globe. The NSA can now track a billion mobile phones and can even access them through the apps to take pictures, video, record data and listen in on conversations. The agency is also responsible for infiltrating technology companies to circumvent internet privacy.

Rulings in the US have deemed these methods of data collection to be legal,

THE NSA

Edward Snowden was responsible for a serious security breach at the NSA

whereas the United Nations has condemned the practice for violating international treaties and basic privacy laws. Director of National Intelligence James Clapper and NSA Director Keith Alexander accepted that telephone data was collected but that conversations and emails were not analysed. Both were forced to retract their comments when it was revealed that the PRISM and XKeyscore systems collected and analysed communications from millions of Americans, although they justified their position by claiming that 54 terrorist attacks had been thwarted having obtained evidence by these means. The NSA's Deputy Director John Inglis then announced that the intercepts hadn't actually prevented any attacks.

The agency is now based at Fort Meade in Maryland and employs approximately 40,000 people. Most are subjected to regular polygraph tests to ensure their allegiance to the United States. The agency also runs several listening stations in America, notably in Denver, Georgia, Hawaii and Salt Lake City, and around the world in North Yorkshire, Morwenstow in Cornwall, three towns in Australia, plus other stations in Canada, Japan and New Zealand.

Chapter 22

Arthur Owens

Arthur Owens was born in Wales in 1899. Having left school he graduated to the head of a company making batteries for ships. He ended up running the business and secured contracts with the Royal Navy and the Kriegsmarine. The Secret Intelligence Service realised he could provide useful information on German shipping in Kiel so they recruited him in 1936.

Two years later, an Abwehr agent in Britain, Nikolaus Ritter, contacted Owens and asked him to provide the Germans with information about the British fleet. Owens was attracted by the money and the women so he gladly turned over his files. However, when he returned to Britain in 1938 he had a change of heart and gave the British his radio transceiver as a show of faith.

He returned to Hamburg just before the outbreak of the Second World War but the British then decided he was playing both sides and brought him in for questioning when he arrived home. He was sent to Wandsworth Prison and forced to commit himself to Britain. Having convinced the British of his allegiance, he was released to travel to Brussels to meet his Abwehr contact.

The Germans were also having doubts about his credibility so they asked Owens to deliver regular weather reports to test him. He seemed to pass their tests so most Abwehr agents visited Owens in Britain. The SIS instructed him to give these enemy agents false names and ration books so they'd soon be apprehended, but they also assigned another

ARTHUR OWENS

ABOVE Arthur Owens was also a double agent with the codename 'Snow'

double agent, Sam McCarthy, to him to make sure he wasn't playing both sides.

Although Owens undoubtedly helped deliver several spies who had entered the country under Operation Lena, McCarthy concluded he was still working for the Germans as he was a slave to the money they were paying.

MI5 imprisoned him on Dartmoor but he continued providing them with information gleaned from the German inmates.

He emigrated to Canada after the war and was paid for his silence after threatening to publish his memoirs. He died in Ireland in 1957.

Chapter 23

Oleg Penkovsky

Oleg Penkovsky was born in North Ossetia in 1919. He graduated from the Kiev Artillery Academy at the age of 20 and reached the rank of lieutenant-colonel fighting the Finns in the Second World War. He then joined the GRU and was posted to Turkey. It is still unknown where Penkovsky's allegiances lay as there are two competing theories.

The first account states that Penkovsky gave some American students in Moscow a package. They delivered it to the CIA but the agency believed he was under surveillance and refused to make contact. Penkovsky then approached British agent Greville Wynne and the pair arranged a meeting with British Intelligence and the CIA in London in 1961.

Penkovsky proved his worth by supplying information about the size and capability of the Soviet nuclear arsenal over the next two years, particularly that the fuelling and guidance systems weren't fully operational. He also supplied maps of the launch sites in Cuba and confirmed that medium-range ballistic missiles were being transported to the island under Operation Anadyr.

British intelligence officer and scientist Peter Wright had a different opinion, however. He believed Penkovsky only gave the West information that was of little value or had already been discovered, and that he never betrayed any Soviet agents in the US or Britain. British Intelligence was being rocked by the Cambridge Five fiasco so the Russians

OLEG PENKOVSKY

ABOVE Oleg Penkovsky

planted Penkovsky to take advantage of the confusion and report back to the Soviet Union about intelligence in the West. Wright also suggests the FBI were suspicious of Penkovsky and believed him to be a plant.

With several former KGB officers naming Penkovsky as a double agent, the first scenario is perhaps more plausible. The Russians put him under surveillance to build up a case against him without having to rely on their sources inside MI6 and the CIA. They arrested him in October 1962 and forced him to contact his American handlers about a dead drop. When the handlers turned up to collect the drop, they too were arrested. Penkovsky was apparently burned alive as a warning against working for the West, although Wright believes he was promoted and kept out of the public eye.

Dušan Popov

Dušan Popov was born to a wealthy family in Titel in 1912, which was then part of Austro-Hungary but which is now in Serbia. He had many German friends and spoke the language fluently but, having been mistreated while at university in Freiburg, he was a staunch anti-Nazi. He earned his PhD in law and returned to Dubrovnik to practise as an attorney.

A friend from university, Johann Jebsen, asked him to work for the Abwehr so he told Clement Hope, a British passport control officer in Yugoslavia, of his intention. Hope recruited Popov as a double agent and the Germans dispatched him to London as an employee of an import-export business. This cover allowed him to take a weekly flight to Lisbon to meet his German handlers, although he only fed them information that was carefully controlled by MI6. He returned with details about German shipping and intelligence gathering that were extremely valuable to the British.

In 1941, the Germans provided Popov with a budget and sent him to America to establish a network of agents. He was also given a questionnaire to help him recruit intelligence officers. An entire page of the form was dedicated to Pearl Harbor so Popov warned the FBI that the Germans were obviously interested in the Hawaiian Islands. There is no record of J Edgar Hoover passing on his concerns, probably because Hoover doubted Popov's credibility. Four months later, the Japanese launched a surprise attack on the American Pacific

DUŠAN POPOV

BELOW Dušan Popov

Fleet at anchor in the harbour.

By 1944, Jebsen was also working for the Allies, but he was eventually betrayed to the Germans. The British thought Popov might be involved but no link was ever proven and he returned to fieldwork after the war. With his import-export cover, lavish lifestyle and eye for the ladies, Popov has been credited with being the man on whom Ian Fleming based James Bond. Popov died in 1981 at the age of 69.

Chapter 25

Sidney Reilly

Sidney Reilly was also suggested as a model for James Bond. He was born Georgi Rosenblum in Odessa in what is now Ukraine but thereafter his life and exploits became shrouded in mystery, much of it fabricated or exaggerated by the man himself. He was arrested in 1892 by the Russian secret police for apparently working for revolutionary groups so he faked his death and fled to Brazil on his release.

Having taken the name Pedro, he was asked to join a British Intelligence expedition as its cook. He then apparently saved the group from a band of hostile natives and was rewarded by the expedition leader, Major Charles Fothergill, with £1,500, a British passport and passage to England.

Andrew Cook's biography disputes this version, however, claiming that he arrived in Britain from France after robbing two Italian anarchists of revolutionary funds.

Now known as Sigmund Rosenblum, he became an informant for Special Branch and entered into an affair with a married woman, Margaret Thomas, whose husband died in mysterious circumstances shortly afterwards. Thomas inherited £800,000 and she and Rosenblum married five months later. The money allowed him to forge a new identity as Sidney George Reilly and travel to Russia and the Far East.

He is said to have looked for oil in the Caucasus and acted as a double agent during the Russo-Japanese War in early 1904. He and a business partner made a fortune supplying both sides with food and raw materials. He also stole the map of the minefield guarding the Russian fleet in Port Arthur, which allowed the Japanese to manoeuvre inside and launch a surprise attack. Both sides suffered heavy casualties.

Reilly was back in Paris in June to meet William Melville, the first head of the Secret Intelligence Service. Melville asked Reilly to find William D'Arcy and have him sell his newly acquired rights to oil reserves in Persia and Mesopotamia to the British rather than the French. Having successfully negotiated the deal under the noses of the Rothschilds on their yacht in the Mediterranean, Reilly stole the ignition magneto from a German aircraft at a show in Frankfurt. In 1909 he was sent back to Germany to steal plans of their weapons, and he supposedly mailed vital information from a

SIDNEY REILLY

shipyard in Essen.

Reilly claimed to have spent much of the First World War behind German lines, but it's more likely he was selling munitions to both sides from an office in New York. When arms sales plummeted in 1917, he joined the Royal Canadian Flying Corps and earned a commission.

The following year, he was back in England and had been recruited as a case officer by the SIS. He was tasked with entering Russia to overthrow the Bolshevik government and assassinate Lenin. Reilly recruited disillusioned Latvian Riflemen who were supposed to guard the Kremlin and lined up Soviet military leaders to assume power after the coup. But things went wrong when a cadet killed Lenin's head of state security, and then Lenin himself was wounded by Fanya Kaplan. Lenin retaliated by rounding up his political opponents and executing them, and, having learned of British involvement, he also raided their embassy in Petrograd where Reilly had his headquarters.

Reilly escaped via Finland and Sweden to London but, despite being sentenced to death *in absentia* by the Soviets, he was back in Russia within a week to assess the divisions of land along the Black Sea coast that had been laid out at the Treaty of Versailles.

He was awarded a Military Cross in 1919 but it wasn't clear whether this was for valour on the frontline or his covert operations behind it. Given all the evidence it seems likely that Reilly worked for whoever paid top dollar, which was usually the British, and that he embellished his considerable achievements with stories that were demonstrably false. His lavish lifestyle, womanising and tendency to lose the trust of important intelligence officers, saw him effectively dismissed from the SIS in 1921.

In 1925, Soviet agents lured Reilly to Russia to meet a fictional anti-communist organisation. He was arrested and taken to Lubyanka Prison where he was interrogated extensively. Reilly refused to crack and documented the entire ordeal on cigarette papers that he hid in his cell. He was taken to a forest outside Moscow in November and executed by firing squad on Stalin's orders. When his captors discovered his 'diaries', they photographed them as a record of their interrogation techniques.

LEFT Sidney Reilly

Julius and Ethel Rosenberg

Julius Rosenberg was born to Jewish immigrants in New York in 1918. He joined the Young Communist League while at college and graduated with a degree in electrical engineering. Ethel Greenglass was also born to a Jewish family in New York in 1915. She initially wanted to perform on stage but eventually took a job at a shipping company and met Julius at the YCL.

Julius worked for the signal corps at Fort Monmouth for the duration of the Second World War but he was fired in 1945 because of his communist leanings. By then, he had already been recruited by the NKVD and had spent three years passing top-secret documents – such as the complete plans for the Lockheed P80 – to the Soviet

JULIUS AND ETHEL ROSENBERG

intelligence agency. He also found time to recruit Joel Barr, Alfred Sarant, Bill Perl and Morton Sobell to his spy ring. When his handler, Alexander Feklisov, learned that Rosenberg's brother-in-law, David Greenglass, was working on the Manhattan Project at Los Alamos, he asked Julius to recruit him as well.

The Americans were extremely surprised at how quickly the Russians were able to conduct a nuclear test and they soon discovered that Klaus Fuchs had been passing them information. Fuchs gave them the name of his courier, Harry Gold, under interrogation, and Gold then implicated Greenglass. He told investigators that Julius had been behind the operation but that Ethel had only typed up the odd document and probably knew nothing of the betrayal.

The conspirators were tried and convicted in 1951, largely on the

LEFT The Rosenbergs are found guilty of espionage

ABOVE They were executed at Sing Sing Prison

JULIUS AND ETHEL ROSENBERG

evidence of David Greenglass who volunteered information to avoid a death sentence. The Rosenbergs were sentenced to death under the 1917 Espionage Act. The sentence was carried out by electric chair at the Sing Sing Correctional Facility in New York on June 19, 1953.

Their contribution to the development of the Soviet Union's A-bomb is debatable: Nikita Krushchev believed they had provided significant information, while several engineers maintain the Rosenbergs gave them nothing of value. Feklisov suggested that the Rosenbergs simply didn't know enough about the weapon itself but did provide valuable electronic data. It took until 2008 before Sobell admitted he had been part of the spy ring.

BELOW Morton Sobell (left) was also part of the spy ring

Chapter 27
Frederick Rutland and William Forbes-Sempill

Britain and Japan were allies in the First World War and they signed a naval treaty with the US in 1922. However, the British refused to let the Japanese study their aircraft carriers, which enraged the Japanese High Command. They eventually reached a compromise because Britain needed arms contracts in the Far East. A civilian mission was organised so that the British were seen to be helping their ally but they never imagined that the Japanese would develop new carrier technology and then break the agreement to take an unassailable naval advantage.

The British chose William Forbes-Sempill to lead the mission. He was an expert pilot with the Royal Flying Corps and the Royal Naval Air Service so he left for Japan in 1920. He showed the Japanese how to increase the effectiveness of their dive bombing and torpedo attacks and also suggested building a fleet of carriers so that their aircraft could be deployed on the other side of the ocean at short notice. Within two years, the Japanese had built their first carrier.

Things changed at the Washington Naval Conference in 1922. Britain and the United States no longer saw each other as the main threat so they tried to restrict the tonnage of Japanese warships. When they refused, Britain severed its ties with Japan and excluded them from further talks, sowing the seeds of mistrust between East and West. These seeds flourished when the Japanese turned Sempill. They still needed

FREDERICK RUTLAND AND WILLIAM FORBES-SEMPILL

pilot training, however, so Semphill suggested approaching Frederick Rutland, squadron leader on Britain's biggest aircraft carrier, *HMS Eagle*.

Rutland, somewhat naively, believed that the superpowers wouldn't risk another war so he left the services and joined Sempill in Japan. As a pioneering ace who'd won the Albert Medal and spotted the German fleet during the Great War, he was assigned to Mitsubishi, then a front for the government. He impressed them with his knowledge of naval aviation, and he trained their airmen to land and take off from the carriers, work that led to the formation of the Japanese Air Arm.

When Sempill returned home, he became involved in arms sales and came to the attention of MI5. In February 1924, Sempill contacted the Japanese attaché in London – intelligence officer Captain Teijirō Toyoda – and gave away top-secret information about bombs that could be used to destroy the enemy's capital ships. The Secret Intelligence Service were already monitoring him so now they tapped his phone. For the next three years, Sempill passed on official

Captain William Forbes-Sempill showing a Gloster Sparrowhawk to Admiral Togo Heihachiro in 1921

FREDERICK RUTLAND AND WILLIAM FORBES-SEMPILL

Sempill at the controls

FREDERICK RUTLAND AND WILLIAM FORBES-SEMPILL

secrets while both he and Toyoda used their connections to try luring British carrier designers and Air Vice-Marshal Sir Charles Vyvyan into their web. MI5 were appalled at this breach of security, even though they'd initially believed that Sempill was only trying to further British interests abroad by securing defence contracts. They decided to keep quiet, however, because blowing Sempill's cover could raise questions about how they'd got their information and might alert the Japanese that they'd deciphered their codes.

Aside from the letters and telephone conversations that could be intercepted, some of the information was exchanged electronically. MI5 decided not to risk giving that advantage away. It was only when

BELOW The Iris flying boat

FREDERICK RUTLAND AND WILLIAM FORBES-SEMPILL

Sempill began haemorrhaging information about the Iris flying boat in 1925 that they decided to act because it was now clear he was being paid for the intelligence. But they didn't want him to know that he'd been under surveillance.

The SIS finally got lucky when Sempill was asked to advise the Greek air force because the Greeks expressed reservations given his dealings with the Japanese. This infuriated Sempill so he requested a meeting with the air ministry. Now the SIS had their chance to question him, but they had to tread carefully. Sempill initially suggested that his connections with the Japanese were inconsequential, but while he was on his way to the Iris factory he had talked openly about the secret project in front of two foreign advisors, a blatant breach of the Official Secrets Act that had been reported by the inspection team.

Sempill was cornered and he knew it, but the story had a few more twists. His father was an aide to King George V and a public trial would have embarrassed the establishment. It would also have revealed the SIS's sources, which could never be made public. The damage had been done, however. In just seven years the Japanese fleet was equal that of the Royal Navy. Throughout the 1930s Sempill worked at the admiralty and continued to pass on sensitive information via Mitsubishi, particularly how their carriers could deliver long-range aircraft strikes against enemy ships.

ABOVE Frederick Rutland

The Secret Service

The United States Secret Service reports to the Department of Homeland Security and is responsible for protecting the current president and his family, plus former presidents, presidential candidates, visiting dignitaries and American embassies abroad. It also works to prevent counterfeiting of federal currency and securities, as well as investigating financial crimes like money laundering, forgery and serious telecommunications fraud. In 2001, President George Bush established an electronic crimes division within the service. It was tasked with preventing cyber attacks on American financial institutions and critical infrastructure. The head of the service is appointed directly by the president.

The agency was formed to combat counterfeiting during the Civil War as approximately a third of all the tender in circulation was believed to be illegal. Secretary of the Treasury Hugh McCulloch appointed William Wood as its first chief and he was sworn in in Washington, DC in 1865. The legislation had to be approved by President Lincoln and the paperwork was on his desk the night he was assassinated by John Wilkes Booth in Ford's Theatre.

As the other enforcement agencies were incapable of dealing with every federal crime, the Secret Service initially investigated everything from murder to robbery, and it was only when President William McKinley became the third president (after Lincoln and James Garfield) to be assassinated in 1901 that it

RIGHT President William McKinley

THE SECRET SERVICE

was assigned to protect future holders of the office. As such, it became the first domestic counterintelligence agency, although the FBI assumed control of this role in 1908.

While the White House was being renovated in 1950, President Truman moved to Blair House. On November 1, two Puerto Ricans tried to break in to assassinate Truman. Oscar Collazo and Griselio Torresola shot Private Leslie Coffelt and members of the Secret Service but, despite being mortally wounded, Coffelt killed Torresola. Coffelt remains the only man to date to die protecting the serving president.

The assassination of President John F Kennedy in Dallas in 1963 exposed shortcomings in the service's training and led to some questioning its effectiveness. The service responded by tightening up its security procedures but, as they hadn't yet been assigned to presidential candidates, they weren't on hand to protect Bobby Kennedy and he too was assassinated in Los Angeles in 1968. (Both candidates and nominees received protection immediately after the shooting.)

When John Hinckley fired six shots in an assassination attempt on Ronald

THE SECRET SERVICE

John Hinckley's assassination attempt on President Ronald Reagan

THE SECRET SERVICE

Reagan in 1981, Agent Tim McCarthy leaped into the line of fire and took a bullet in the stomach. Reagan was rushed to George Washington Memorial Hospital but recovered from bullet wounds to his chest and arm. Press Secretary James Brady was paralysed during the attack and eventually died from complications three decades later. Despite the injuries sustained by the immediate personnel, quick thinking by the Secret Service undoubtedly saved Reagan's life, although more had to be done to ensure the safety of the commander in chief.

The service now employs around 7,000 staff in 136 field offices and has an annual budget of nearly two billion dollars. Its duties have recently been expanded to run security at designated events, protect foreign heads of state on official visits to the US, establish overseas bases to monitor cyber-crime and identity theft, and manage its own uniformed division of close-protection officers. Special Agents are highly trained in weapons and unarmed combat and are required to meet exacting levels of physical and mental fitness.

John Hinckley. He may soon be released from prison having served 35 years

Richard Sorge

Richard Sorge was born near Baku in what is now Azerbaijan in 1895. His German father was a mining engineer but, when his contract in the Caucasus expired, he moved his Russian wife and nine children back to Berlin. Sorge signed up to the field artillery to fight for Germany in the First World War but he was seriously injured on the Western Front in 1916 and was dispatched after receiving the Iron Cross.

He studied Marxism and economics during his recovery and then joined the Communist Party of Germany, a position that saw him fired from two jobs. He promptly moved to the Soviet Union and joined the Comintern. He was soon recruited to Soviet Intelligence and he travelled around Europe posing as a journalist while gathering information on the influence of communism. By 1929 he was seconded to the Red Army's Fourth Department, which later became the GRU. Later that year he visited London with orders to assess the strength of the Communist Party of Great Britain. He also infiltrated the Nazi Party in Berlin and then worked undercover in Shanghai, developing contacts with Chinese communists and relaying news of the escalating Chinese-Japanese conflict.

In 1933 Sorge was sent back to the Far East to establish an intelligence network in Japan. Over the next year he renewed old contacts and formed a network of informants, radio operators and ex-military personnel. He also

RICHARD SORGE

gained access to politicians and sensitive foreign policy documents. From these he learned about the pact between Japan and the Nazis, and he also discovered that Germany was planning to invade the Soviet Union in June 1941 under the codename Barbarossa. He tried to warn Moscow but Stalin ignored the evidence.

When Sorge provided detail about

ABOVE Superspy Richard Sorge

RICHARD SORGE

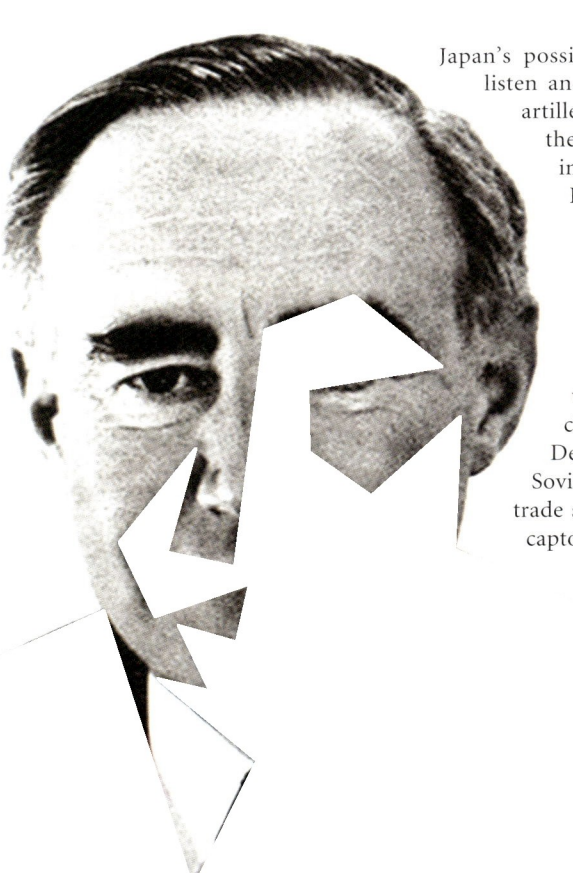

Japan's possible attack in the east, Stalin was forced to listen and he was able to relocate many infantry and artillery divisions. This allowed him to overwhelm the Germans during the Battle of Moscow and inflict the first tactical defeat on the Nazis after Barbarossa. The Japanese realised they must have an intelligence operation undermining their war effort so the secret police began to close in on Sorge and his accomplices.

With several of his team already in custody, Sorge was arrested for espionage in October 1941. At first, the Japanese thought he'd been working for the Germans but it soon became clear that his allegiance lay with the Russians. Despite Sorge's confession under torture, the Soviets denied any knowledge of him and refused to trade spies with the Japanese. He was hanged by his captors in Sagumo Prison in November 1944.

Twenty years later, the Soviets finally admitted that Sorge had been working for them and they made him a Hero of the Soviet Union. He is even said to have recruited British agent Roger Hollis, a man who would become director of MI5 for nine years during the Cold War. Despite several investigations into Hollis's life, no credible evidence surfaced that he was a Soviet agent. Sorge is said by many informed authors, intelligence officers and politicians to be the greatest spy of all time.

James Bond

No book on secret agents would be complete without mentioning fictional spies, and James Bond is surely the most famous agent to grace the silver screen. Author Ian Fleming worked for naval intelligence during the Second World War and he later admitted that Bond was a mosaic of several people he met and worked with, including his brother Peter and the Ace of Spies, Sidney Reilly, although he based Bond's looks on himself and American singer Hoagy Carmichael.

Fleming spent several English winters in the West Indies and he took the name of his hero from the author of a field guide to the birds of the islands, saying that he wanted the character to have a boring name, but to whom extraordinary things would happen. As so often seems to be the case, authors give their characters many of their own traits and Bond was no exception, sharing Fleming's golf handicap, love of gambling, eye for the ladies and a penchant for fine wine and other exotic drinks.

In early 1952, Fleming wrote *Casino Royale* at his hilltop estate in Jamaica known as Goldeneye. The manuscript was initially rejected by Jonathan Cape but Peter Fleming, by then an established travel writer, eventually convinced Cape to publish the book, the first of 12 novels and two short-story collections. (Kingsley Amis, John Gardner, Raymond Benson and Sebastian Faulks, amongst others, continued the series after Fleming's death in 1964.)

Casino Royale was a moderate success

JAMES BOND

Ian Fleming

so Fleming penned another thriller every winter. He soon settled into a rhythm of planning, writing and editing, and Cape continued publishing the results. Bond may have languished in relative obscurity had President Kennedy not listed *From Russia With Love* as one of his favourite books. Thereafter, Bond began his own quest for world domination.

A year after *Casino Royale* was published, CBS paid Fleming $1,000 for the rights to adapt it as a one-off TV special with Barry Nelson in the title role. In 1956, *Moonraker* was aired as a radio broadcast in South Africa with Bob Holness playing Bond, but it wasn't until Harry Saltzman and Cubby Broccoli's Eon Productions bought the rights to *Doctor No* and installed Sean Connery as Bond that the character finally arrived on the big screen. The producers weren't confident in the project, however, so they only allocated it a budget of $1 million. It took $60 million at the box office and, by the time *Goldfinger* was unleashed two years later, Bond had become a global phenomenon, although Fleming was in poor health and died just before the film's release.

He'd initially been critical of Connery's interpretation of Bond but, hav-

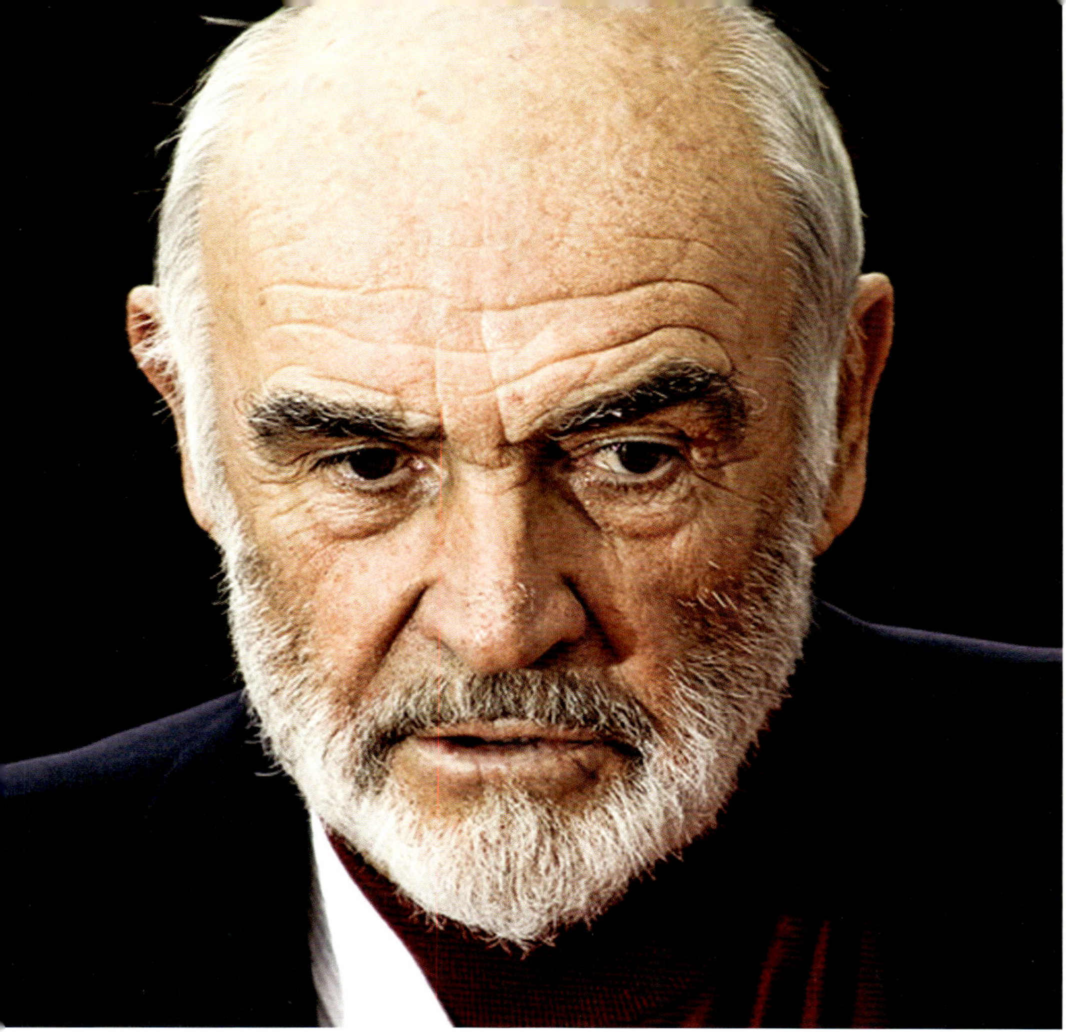

ing been impressed with the first two films, Fleming added a backstory in later novels that included Bond's Scottish roots. By the time Connery had finished filming *Thunderball* in 1965, he felt the press intrusion into his private life was unmanageable and, despite the huge success of the franchise, he committed to one more film. *You Only Live Twice* only retained the Far Eastern locations from the original book as it was felt Bond's inner torment and personal duel with Blofeld wouldn't translate to the big screen. Instead, the Roald Dahl-penned screenplay almost took Bond into outer space, a change in direction so drastic that Bond purists felt that Eon had sold out purely to make a fast buck.

With Connery not prepared to reprise the role, unknown Australian actor George Lazenby stepped into the breach for *On Her Majesty's Secret Service*, one of the best books (to which the screenplay remained largely faithful). However, audiences didn't warm to Lazenvy, and the film's downbeat ending – praised by purists – alienated those new to Bond. Eon pulled out all the stops and convinced Connery to return in *Diamonds Are Forever*. Despite a weaker script and Connery's obvious reluctance to continue in the role, the gamble paid off and the franchise was rescued from the brink of extinction.

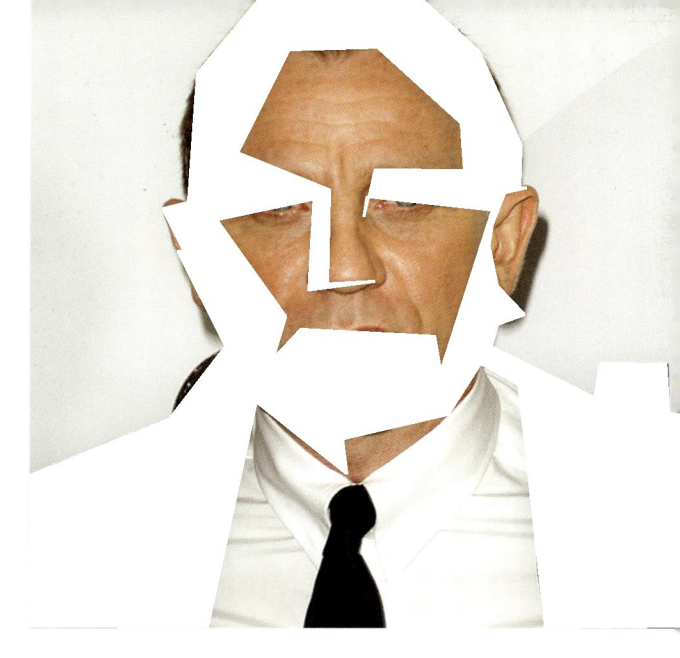

Half a century, 23 Eon films and six lead actors later, Bond has grossed more than $6 billion worldwide and spawned countless imitators and spin-offs. With his quick wit, outrageous gadgets, exotic cocktails, knack of attracting gorgeous women and defeating the villains with style and panache, Bond, somewhat counterintuitively, remains the most recognisable secret agent in the world.

LEFT Sean Connery brought Bond to the masses in the first feature film, Dr No (1962)

ABOVE Daniel Craig is the latest actor to play James Bond

All images in this book are copyright and have been provided courtesy of the following:

WIKICOMMONS
commons.wikimedia.org

Design & Artwork: ALEX YOUNG

Published by: DEMAND MEDIA LIMITED

Publisher: JASON FENWICK

Written by: LIAM McCANN